THE **HOWLING** OF **MEMORY**

ASKEW'S
WORD ON THE **LAKE**
ANTHOLOGY
2023

FICTION, NONFICTION,
AND POETRY FROM
CONTEST WINNERS
AND
PRESENTERS

Cover photo by and copyright Shirley DeKelver

Design and typography by (studio)Effigy

Edited by Scott Fitzgerald Gray

The Word on the Lake Writers' Festival is a nonprofit celebration of the written word, organized and presented annually by the Shuswap Association of Writers. All sales of the *Askew's Word on the Lake Anthology 2023* go directly toward supporting Word on the Lake.

TABLE OF CONTENTS

From the **Shuswap Association of Writers**

On behalf of the Shuswap Association of Writers, I would like to thank all the contestants who entered this year's Askew's Word on the Lake Writing Contest. While the last few years have been challenging — with one festival cancelled, one presented by Zoom, and one change of location — the writing contest organizers have continued to persevere in difficult circumstances to keep a healthy contest alive.

This is the tenth year that we have offered the contest, to encourage, promote, and reward writers not just from our local area but from across Canada, and it is also a milestone twentieth anniversary of the festival. A special thank you goes to our judges, who gave generously of their time to adjudicate the many entries in three categories: nonfiction, poetry, and fiction.

We would also like to thank Askew's Foods, who became the sole sponsor of the contest at its creation ten years ago, and who have continued to support the contest ever since.

This year, we also wish to thank Simon Fraser University and the Writer's Studio at SFU for their donation of three online creative writing courses for the first-place winners in each category.

I must also thank Mary-Lou McCausland and Virginia McCausland for starting the writing contest and the *Word on the Lake Anthology*, and Scott Fitzgerald Gray for his work the last four years to make the contest a continued success, and for expanding the anthology in both print and e-book formats.

This year, the Word on the Lake planning committee are looking forward to presenting our anniversary festival in Salmon Arm again, at the Prestige Harbourfront Resort and the Salmon Arm Campus of Okanagan College.
We have a full slate of presenters and entertainers planned, with many favourites from past events, and look forward to a fun celebratory weekend.

Best regards,

Debra Turner
Shuswap Association of Writers

FROM OUR **CONTEST SPONSOR**
ASKEW'S

For two decades, the Shuswap has hosted the annual Word on the Lake Writers' Festival. This festival serves to encourage new, emerging, and seasoned writers to celebrate the full diversity of the written word, and the gifted writers who guide us in our exploration through their stories and poetry.

Through the years, Askew's has stayed true to its founding principles of fostering community by providing value, contributing to the health of our community, and dedication and goodwill. We believe our sponsorship of the Word on the Lake Writing Contest since its inception as part of the festival ten years ago serves the purpose of providing value to our general community by supporting our creative community, which then contributes to the sharing of creativity and knowledge. The sharing of creativity can then produce goodwill by establishing a sense of connection with the listening, reading, and writing audience.

Askew's ongoing presence in the community for the past ninety-four years has given us the opportunity to help support Salmon Arm's rich population of writers and storytellers through sponsorship of this festival, which we are proud to support.

David Askew,
President and CEO,
Askew's Foods

Write what should not be forgotten.

— Isabel Allende

HEH DIDDLEY DEE, THE **WRITER'S LIFE** FOR ME! OR: ACCEPTING THE **MONSTER WITHIN**

CHRIS (C.C.) HUMPHREYS

I thought I'd talk a little about the writer's life.

Or rather *this* writer's life. Not in the full autobiographical sense. You'll have to wait for my autobiography, which will be published posthumously, as my plan is to punish anyone who has ever stood in my way. Critics will be criticized, editors stringently edited, rivals savaged — especially the ones who are far more successful than I! I will not care because I will be dead! Revenge is a dish best eaten cold, they say, and there's nothing colder than the grave.

No, I was thinking about the many ways that writing impacts on my day, every day. Because from the moment I wake until the lights go out again, there is some aspect of everything I do that will have to do with writing. Most writers — those who dedicate their lives to the craft, the business, the agony, and the occasional ecstasy — are never entirely off the clock. Even their dreams are resources for images and words that will occupy the subsequent day.

For example, I am a runner. I run for fitness, sure. But a major reason is that it is a huge part of my writing process. I take ideas on a run — sowing seeds for a future project or fixing an issue that has arisen in my work-in-progress. Hithertofore (I like that word, even if I just made it up; it's almost Germanic in its multi-syllable-ality) I have written whole poems on a run. I have also, on many occasions, come up with solutions that completely changed the course of a novel. And it is not even that I spend the whole time thinking about writing. Mostly I am studying the ground ahead, so I don't trip and fall, something I am prone to do (and prone *once* I do!). Yet, in the forests and by the rivers and seas, writing is what happens. I have been known to start sprinting on the homeward stretch, desperate to seize pen and pad and jot down the new ideas before they vanish.

For writing is not a 9-to-5 job. It can happen at any hour, day, or night. Once you've accepted that you are a writer — and, trust me, that can take a long time; I didn't truly consider my-self one until my fifth or sixth novel had been published — you quite quickly realize that you have made a pact with the Devil. In exchange for your soul, you have been given a way of noting down your experience in the world — with the additional com-mandment that *it must be shared*. You must also accept that you will never be free of the obsession.

There's a story about a writer and his wife. They've just had their first baby and they are in the sleepless phase. The baby wakes at 2:47 a.m., screams. Keeps screaming because no one comes. Finally the wife jabs her elbow into her husband's back.

"It's your turn," she hisses.

"Shh," he replies. "I'm writing."

That may have been me. At the very least, I sympathize. Because in order to write, writers must, at some base level of their DNA, be monsters. Though selfishness may be the least egregious of one's monstrous qualities. It's the vampiric that I am most aware of. That little part of the writer's brain that is noting down experience, any experience, at the moment they are having it. Stacking the logs for the fires of future scribblings. I have had terrible rows, when I am passionately and emotionally defending myself, my point of view… while simultaneously *writing it down in my head*. What can be worse is that there is often some instant editing going on. I have played what Bob Seger ("Hollywood Nights") calls "the famous final scene." Broken up with a girlfriend, say. There were tears, shortness of breath, heartstrings snapping… and all the while I am noting down the *bloody specifics*!

I acknowledge that it is not a healthy way to live. Though the running — and the tai chi which I also practice — do provide ancillary benefits. And it is not like I don't experience the emotions. I do commit to them in the moment. Though of course, since I am an actor, committing to emotions in the moment is my stock in trade. Yet in almost any situation, it does feel as if there are two of me engaged in the actions. There's Jekyll. Yet Hyde is always there too. Grinning, he hefts a pen.

One other issue with being a writer is *not* writing. It's all very well to be a vampire, feasting on the blood of others. Vampires have their justifications, right? They must feed to live. So at some point, a writer must transform their experience into those odd little swirls and curlicues that we call words. For if you do not? Well then, all that time spent not being entirely present with loved ones simply cannot be justified, even by the lame excuse of "art." Which is why I recommend the Humphreys Method. Summed up in the phrase: "Writing is *Writing*." Don't angst about it, don't pre-judge it, don't beat yourself up about this essential flaw in your human nature. Accept your monster status, say goodbye to Heaven… and write.

For as James Joyce said, "Write, you fool! What else are you good for?"

(Slightly adapted from one of the essays I wrote on Medium, the online publishing platform. To follow me there and read other essays — including the ones I wrote while travelling for three months last year in Europe — go here: https://medium.com/@c.c.humphreys*)*

MEMORY ALLEY

FINNIAN BURNETT

For the thousandth time, I'm contemplating leaving David, when he tells me he finally found a service that allows you to change the things that happened in your past. *I gave them our life savings*, he says, and I'm not mad that he hadn't talked to me first because we never talk to each other anymore and I'm not even mad about the money because the only thing I'd been saving for was Stewart's college.

We can go back as far as we want, David says, *but we have to go together*. He pauses, shuffles his feet. *It was the only condition.*

He's afraid I'll say no. We've been together long enough I can read him. He can read me too, and I know my simmering hatred has stabbed at him from my glaring eyes, crossed arms, from my unyielding back turned on him in our bed.

I don't ask what he had to do to find this service, who he had to kill, what dark places he had to visit. I don't care how much of his soul he had to sell. I don't ask because I don't care. I don't ask because I know, even without his words, without his imploring face, how far back he wants to go. Not to when he got kicked out of college for cheating on his midterms, or that time I got drunk at the Bensons' Christmas party and stuck my tongue down Harold Benson's throat behind the coat rack and after, David and I had a fight in which we both mentioned divorce at least once. No, not then.

He says we must be there at exactly 11:17 p.m. on the night of the Sturgeon Moon. We consult the Internet and realize we have to wait more than six months, six months I have to spend staring at his gloomy face and listening to his bullshit apologies. But David doesn't apologize for six months. Instead, he spends the time trying to convince me it's the right thing to do, the only thing to do, until I scream at him to shut up because of course it's the right thing to do and what's the alternative? Hate each other until one of us dies?

On the night of the Sturgeon Moon, we stand on a street in the warehouse district at 11:16, staring at a nondescript building where David says the person told him to go.

It appears at the exact time, he says, though his voice cracks and he sounds unsure.

For a second, I lose hope. It was a scam. David spent our life savings on a dream. But my phone shows 11:17 and the streetlights go out and a gaping maw opens between the buildings.

Now, David yells, and we rush through before it can close, before we can change our minds.

We're in an alley and David propels me forward with a strong hand at my elbow. We speed walk through darkness, but shapes coalesce from the shadows and the shapes form people. In another minute, I realize the people are us — me eating leftover plain pasta from the fridge in the middle of the night, David sadly masturbating in the bathroom, me crying on the floor of the sewing room.

We move faster, and the other couple, the other David and Lorna, scream at each other in the baby department of a crowded department store and they're eating oatmeal silently while David's mom cleans around them. Shadow Lorna sits on a tiny bed, holding a much-repaired stuffed animal. David and Lorna sit in the pews of a church — pale, shell-shocked faces turned away from each other.

There's my mother, curled into bed around me, holding me, holding the other Lorna as she screams and shakes, there's David's father clearing his throat and trying to find words, and there's David apologizing over and over and the police cruiser and the tow truck company and the emergency room doctor and I'm sprinting now to get past this part, past David looking down to text a woman he's considering fucking and he's smiling in a way he hasn't smiled at me in years and I put on a burst of speed because David's sending a text and Stewart is strapped beside him not in the backseat because he's a big boy now and he wants to sit next to his dad.

David gasps next to me, struggling to keep up and we're beyond the accident, beyond the day David destroyed me. I'm still running, running by Stewart's first day of kindergarten and that time he dropped a snake in the bathtub with me and the way his face was all smooshed when he was born and I'd thought, for a brief, unforgivable moment, that he was ugly.

Lorna, you have to stop, David yells, but I can't. I'm sprinting past the night we quietly made love in his dorm bed, the night he took off his shoes and danced in the fountain on campus, the night I got drunk on Jack Daniels and puked in his lap. I speed up as he struggles for breath next to me past a million happy smiles and a thousand tiny emotional cuts, and by the time he catches me, we haven't gotten married, he hasn't dropped out of college, we haven't even met.

We're standing on a street in front of a nondescript building in the warehouse district, me and a good-looking man with mousy brown hair and a slight gap in his front teeth. Before my mother's voice can pop in my head, *stranger danger*, I'm smiling, and the man smiles back.

"I'm David," he says, and his voice is a lullaby, a love song, a long kiss goodnight. It's almost familiar.

I stare at him for a moment and finally, I reach for his hand. "I'm Lorna," I say. "It's nice to meet you."

Second Place — Fiction

This story feels very true to so many relationships that have gone on too long and where the couple are unable to end them. The voice of the narrator is strong, clear, and there is a decent-size shock that reveals why the blame here runs especially deep. The flashbacks, where we see how these people found each other, why they fell in love, are unusual, varied, and true, while the ending is genuinely poignant. It feels universal, because everyone can relate to how a relationship can go really wrong because of accidents and the choices people make, both little and big. Yet we can also look back to a moment, to a feeling, when everything was sunny, and anything was possible.

— Chris (C.C.) Humphreys

WALTZ TIME

KAIJA PEPPER

Professor and Mrs. W.E. O'Brien, among the first dance teachers to set up shop in my hometown, were still alive in the decade in which I was born. Mrs. W.E., or Gertrude, died in 1951, before my time, but I might well have crossed paths with the Professor, who lived until 1957. That is how young Vancouver is, how young its cultural life.

Of course, I would have been a toddler carried, or pushed in a buggy, by my mother. And Mom would not have known who the old man was, or been interested in uncovering his past: for her, Vancouver was all about the future. When she moved here in the 1940s, leaving behind the Alberta farm where she grew up to travel across the mountains to the British Columbia coast, it was in pursuit of exciting modern life.

She found work as a secretary at a bank in downtown Vancouver. On her way to catch a streetcar home at the end of the day, she would head up Granville Street, basking in the glow from the vivid cityscape of neon signs pointing the way to cafés, movie theatres, and the Commodore Ballroom.

The O'Briens arrived in 1893 from Ontario, when Vancouver was just seven years old, joining about fifteen thousand others who were putting their faith in the rapidly growing city. They found a home for their Academy of Dancing and Deportment on the top floor of the recently opened British Columbia Land and Investment Agency Building, on the southeast corner of Homer and Hastings Streets. The school was so popular that the building became known as O'Brien Hall.

In addition to separate classes for "ladies, gentlemen, or juveniles," Gertrude and William hosted evening socials, bringing people together in couple dances such as waltzes, minuets, and polkas. They also taught lancers (a type of quadrille, or square dance) set to John Freeman Davis's sheet music, *Great Pacific Lancers*, composed to honour the addition, in 1871, of British Columbia to the confederation of Canadian provinces.

As a young girl, I learned two of the dances taught by the O'Briens: the minuet, in ballet class, and the waltz, at elementary school. In the 1890s, both were necessary social skills for parlours and ballrooms. By the 1960s, when I learned them, it was for year-end concerts.

Partnered in a ballet-styled minuet with my best friend Wendy, I tried hard to promenade and pas de bourrée with correct form, feeling exposed in a short canary-yellow tutu (my knobby knees, especially).

A year before, the boys' gym class had joined our girls' class so we could form boy-girl couples for the waltz. This was a welcome change from dodging volleyballs and vaulting over a hurdle called the horse but, in reality, a hard beast of wood and leather. Waltzing meant face-to-face, hand-in-hand, ground-level connection in reassuring 3/4 time. My partner, a boy I didn't know, turned out to be a good match, and we were asked to perform in the annual Nights of Music concert.

Onstage in a green chiffon dress with a sash tied in a bow at the back, I stood facing him, not daring eye contact as cellular-level panic at being the centre of attention sent adrenaline coursing through my blood, unsettling my centre of gravity. Once the music began and the dancing commenced, balance was restored as joy crept in through the soles of my feet.

A whirl of waltzes, quadrilles, and mazurkas take place during a magnificently narrated ballroom scene in *Anna Karenina*, when love is variously lost and found by Anna, Kitty, and Count Vronsky. Leo Tolstoy's novel was first published in serial form between 1875 and 1877, almost two decades before the O'Briens arrived in Vancouver, and long before my mother, let alone me, was even born. Yet the story lies closer to home than its setting — so distant in time and place — might suggest.

At the time of publication, my maternal great-grandfather, Luka Sidoroff, was a young man living in a village, Perehod, about two hundred miles south of St. Petersburg, where the fictional Anna Karenina lived. To supplement the family's crops, Luka often worked in a St. Petersburg factory.

As the descendant of serfs, Luka is unlikely to have read *Anna Karenina*'s lengthy tale of the social elite: "high-born," he would have called them, far above his own "low-born" status. I'm not even sure he could read and write; my grandmother — Palegea, who married Luka's eldest son Feodor — couldn't. In my childhood autograph book, Palegea signed her name with three spidery Xs, each stroke of the pen charting a line from her life to mine, from past to present, from Russia to the Canadian farm where she immigrated as a mother of five. (Two more children had died as babies, left behind in their graves.)

Tolstoy allows me to make the journey in the other direction: from the present to the past, from my life in Canada to hers in Russia. With family connections and history lost through revolution and immigration, through language (my grandparents did not speak much English), and through the not inconsiderable distance between rural Alberta and urban Vancouver, much of what I know about Russia has come from its novelists.

Their books also helped me understand my temperamental Russian mother. That is how I have always thought of her, as Russian, though she was an infant in her mother's arms when the family escaped the Bolshevik revolution in 1923, hiding in the bottom of a boat en route to China.

Eventually, the family established a farm outside Hines Creek. Many neighbours were from the old country: they spoke Russian together; ate cabbage rolls and piroshki; drank well-aged homemade braga at parties, when the men danced, dropping to the floor and kicking their legs Cossack-style.

William and Gertrude O'Brien closed their academy in 1930. Their future, in the form of a thriving dance school, had come and gone; a different present was taking society forward. Studios with new energies from concert forms like ballet and tap were booming.

The four-storey building where they had established their school was demolished in 1940, replaced by a sleek rectangular box housing a branch of the Bank of Montreal. A few years later, and a few blocks west, my mother found work at a different bank.

In Vancouver, she met my Finnish father. Like Mom, he had immigrated at a young age, but grew up surrounded by Finns in Port Arthur, now part of Thunder Bay, Ontario. I suppose I should call my parents Finnish Canadian, Russian Canadian, but we didn't double-barrel nationality in those days, taking the Canadian part for granted.

As a child with two very different ancestries, I was brought up to think of myself as, simply, Canadian. That was the future in my parents' eyes, and in mine, too, before I discovered how thinly Canadian soil lies across this colonized land. Yet, having no real connections in either ancestral country — Russia, with President Putin's barbaric aggression in Ukraine, feels farther away than ever, and a childhood pen pal is my sole contact in Finland — I find myself searching for a past here in Canada, in the city where I was born.

The waltz, of course, survived the decades, although today it follows little of the style or etiquette taught at the O'Briens' academy. Or as found at Tolstoy's ball. Except for competitive ballroom dancing, lessons are hardly necessary; most people manage to get through a turn or two when the occasion demands.

Somehow, my parents knew what to do when they opened the floor on their fiftieth wedding anniversary in 2001, the only time I ever saw them dancing together. Mom, in a scarlet and black full-length gown bought for the celebration, entered the space with small, determined steps, a bashful smile lighting her face as she looked up at her husband. He was a shy man who could probably have done without such a public display, but, manfully, Dad took Mom in his arms.

An anniversary waltz is about celebrating the past: as they stepped in time to the tune played by a violinist who appeared from out of the shadows, they might have been pondering their early years as a couple on an evening out, strolling along Granville Street under the friendly glow of neon signage that made every night look like party night. By then, only a few of the signs remained, considered vintage, a reminder of the past.

Now, though I still see my parents cradled in the full and present moment of their duet, they are gone too. The past will dog our heels, the future beguiles, but it's only during the equally elusive time in between that hearts beat and breath flows.

First Place — **Nonfiction**

This is a beautifully nuanced piece of writing, exploring the liminal spaces between past and present, a city's cultural history, and a family's personal history. A dance form takes the reader through its memories, its crisp steps, one two three, one two three, carrying us easily across the pages, the writer's language rich with its music.

— Theresa Kishkan

ROWING

EVAN J

My father is digging
for a memory, drinking bad black rum
not for taste but for nostalgia. My father
he is a barrel of muscle at my table,
sturdier now at sixty
than any year of his youth, a mammoth
in my kitchen stacking two-ton tall tales
with nothing but lone brawn. He tells me

he worked with his hands like his old man,
replaced the ocean for the plains,
cod for an arc welder,
fishing nets for acetylene.
Yet they both gained the same holes in the skin,
the same scars. My father

he tells me about a storm
and jumps onto a shore forty years away
watching a dory come over the bay,
his Nanny, a saint, seated high in the spray,
his Poppy rowing alone

levering oars into the violent wet
like prying stones
from a garden. Building a pile.
The man would grab at a swell,
toss it behind, inhale down
into the trough for an unseen minute
before the next cresting, the
exhalation, one hill closer.
All this to come for dinner.
All this rowing. My father

he is drunk and visiting
after our meal. Outside, now
it is the prairies
and so it's a blizzard. I say,
the drifts in the yard
are like whitecaps. And he nods.

First Place — **POETRY**

An intricate blend of memory and family resurrection, the accompanying words carry a reader into a temporary state of showing impermanence on a landscape. The poem is so fraught with the fragility of human emotion and captures such a visceral image of a world responding to society's imposition. The careful wording in this poem shows such delicate care towards poetry as a craft, and the minimalism speaks volumes. Comparing former family homes and areas to ones where people end up tell the unique stories of diaspora of people over time to search for better futures for one's community. The line "the drifts in the yard/are like whitecaps" perfectly encompasses this. I found myself going back to this poem over and over again.

— Conor Kerr

Hell **Inc.**

Andrew Buckley

"You are ready for this! You are the man! You are strong and you are qualified and you're going to go out there and get that job!"

Trevor's reflection looked back at him with a serious amount of doubt. Sadly, his reflection was nothing special. His curly hair always looked like it was making an attempt to flee from his head, and Trevor was painfully aware he was scrawny and slightly funny-looking, often being described by his college friends as *the one over there that looks like an escaped scarecrow.*

Today's job fair, in Trevor's mind, was his chance to rise higher in the world. He was tired of being a second-rate college student with no income. He wanted more! Today he would become a second-rate college student with a moderately-above-minimum-wage income. He would go to the job fair being held in the college common room — the one that always smelled like burned fish — he would display his resume, and he would say proudly and confidently, "I am Trevor Meldew, I am a hard worker, and you should hire me!"

Trevor's reflection looked unimpressed.

"I can do this," said Trevor, straightening his red tie — the only tie he owned.

He'd bought it to use as a blindfold on his girlfriend in order to spice things up in the bedroom. No sooner had Trevor suggested it as a good idea, in what he considered to be a sexy and seductive manner, than Kelly had pepper sprayed him.

Trevor later concluded this as a perfect summation of his life. Anytime he tried to make any sort of headway, try something new, and make a positive change, life would pepper spray him.

Not today, though! Oh no, not today. "Today I step forth into that hall as the man that everyone will want to hire."

Trevor's reflection, dressed exactly like Trevor in a white shirt, tie, and beige pants, looked so doubtful, it was bordering on sleepy.

Grabbing the leaflet for the job fair from where he'd stuck it in the side of the mirror, he straightened his tie one more time so it was now actually slightly off kilter, and turned away from his reflection. Glancing back over his shoulder, he said, "When we meet again, we will be a member of the workforce. We'll be able to afford to, you know, eat again, and buy important things like booze and underwear."

Trevor grabbed his stack of freshly printed resumes and looked over the scant amount of information. What he lacked in experience, he was certain he'd made up for in his choice of font. It wasn't just Helvetica, it was Helvetica Neue Ultralight *Italic*! And Trevor could not have been prouder.

Striding across his messy dorm room, Trevor swung open the door and stepped with confidence across the threshold, into the dorm hallway where the Eastern European kid whose name no one could pronounce slammed into him, spilling coffee all over the place.

Thirty minutes later, Trevor emerged once more, a stack of slightly creased and crinkled resumes in his hands, stained brown by coffee, and hastily dried with a hair dryer because Trevor's printer was out of ink. He now wore white pants and a bright-blue shirt that clashed angrily with the red tie that was now a darker red, thanks to the aforementioned coffee incident. The clash of colors was so powerfully loud that dogs near the campus began to whimper, but Trevor was determined. No minor coffee-soaking incident by Chengzingunajar — Chezin-gungajur — Chazingjur — the Eastern European kid with the name no one could pronounce, would dampen his spirits or his determination.

"Mildew, you look like a prat!" shouted a nameless voice somewhere in the throng of students.

But Trevor's confidence was relentless. This would be his day! Employment awaited!

"I'm sorry," said the woman with oversized glasses and a disturbing beehive hairstyle, "you're just not qualified."

"To work the fry station at Burgers, Burgers, Burgers?" said Trevor in disbelief.

The woman adjusted her ample frame in the metal folding chair, which let out a small, nearly indiscernible whine. "To hold a position at Burgers, Burgers, Burgers, store number seven hundred and thirty-four, is not just about having a job, it's about saving the world, one burger at a time."

"You're shitting me?" said Trevor.

The woman made a *hmph* sort of noise and slid the coffee-stained resume back across the table. "I just don't think you're Burgers, Burgers, Burgers material."

Trevor picked up the resume, slid it back into his pile, and turned from the table. The job fair was not shaping up the way he expected. Walking into the hall full of bustling, well-dressed students milling around tables of recruiters from various fields of industry had only stoked his determination.

The hall was rectangular in nature, with hardwood floors that had long ceased to carry any lustre and brick walls that had been graffitied and painted over so many times that they no longer remembered what their natural color had been. A floor-to-ceiling mirror had been fitted against one of the walls in the fond hope people wouldn't graffiti it, but all it did was encourage students to be more creative. One exchange student from the depths of some southern subcontinent had caused quite the ruckus when he'd etched a series of troubling symbols into the mirror, while others simply attacked it with a sharpie.

Trevor glanced at the mirror on his way in and gave his reflection a wave. His reflection waved back, but far less enthusiastically.

Trevor had started his job search at the top, applying to tech support companies. After all, he had lots of experience turning computers on and off, and then back on again.

"I am Trevor Meldew, I am a hard worker, and you sh —"

"Let me stop you right there," said the man with just the single eyebrow dominating an unusually square-shaped head. "We're looking for a specific type of person and I don't think it's you."

As it turned out, they were looking for students in the computer science program, and the knowledge that Trevor was enrolled in a smattering of completely unrelated courses because he hadn't the faintest idea what he wanted to do with his life had left them feeling less than confident in his ability to push a button and Google things.

Next, he'd tried the retail stores.

"What did you say?" said the skinny woman with jet-black straight hair, too much makeup, and a red dress that looked like it was crying for attention.

"I didn't say anything yet," said Trevor. "Well, I'm… uh… I'm looking for a job, I'm Trevor Meldew, I'm a —"

"That's great and everything," said the woman as she filed her nails, "but you didn't need to speak words. I could tell from your clothing choice that retail is not in your future. You see, your shirt is screaming at me from behind that terrible excuse for a tie. It's saying 'Don't hire me to sell clothing because I'm a colour-blind moron with the fashion sense of a weasel that lives in the sewers.' "

"My shirt said all that?" said Trevor.

"Yes, it's a very chatty shirt," said the woman, barely sparing him another glance. "Now run along."

And run along Trevor did, to the grocery store table. Trevor was well versed in food. After all, he'd been eating food since he was a baby.

He slid his resume across the table and proclaimed, "My name is Trevor Meldew, I am a hard worker, and you should hire me!"

The man behind the table looked positively captivated. He wore a collared t-shirt and had a face like an excited monkey. "Well that was an introduction!" said the man.

Trevor beamed in a way that the sun does not, in that it was a solid effort, but failed on most accounts. It wasn't really his fault, Trevor was biologically incapable of beaming.

"So, tell me," said the man, a conspiring look on his face like they were both in on some sort of private joke, "why are you, Trevor Meldew, the right person to work at Kwik-E-Mart?"

Trevor opened his mouth and then closed it again. *Think, Trevor! Why do you want to work at a grocery store?* "I love fruit?" he blurted out.

"Oh good, good, excellent! I too love fruit. Oh, how I love fruit, Trevor. You have no idea how much I love fruit," said the man.

"Um, okay, well yeah. Fruit's great."

"You and I are going to have some fun, Trevor. I love a good kumquat. And you, you will be the newest kumquat in my display in the fruit and vegetable section at Kwik-E-Mart!"

This was all getting a bit weird. Trevor believed people should be passionate about things they liked, but this all felt like it was going a bit far. "I'm not exactly sure what to say?"

"Nothing more to say. Together, you and I will share the tantalizing tastes of fresh mangoes, we'll drool over the pomegranate seeds as they burst in our mouths —"

"Yeah, I think I'm just going to go," said Trevor, snatching up his resume.

The man reached across the desk and took hold of Trevor's tie. "Think of the ripening bananas, Trevor! Think of them!"

"I'd rather not, if it's all the same to you." Trevor yanked the tie from the man's grip and ducked into the crowd.

The words "Come back, my kumquat!" died in the noise of the crowd as Trevor hurried on to the fast-food section.

He couldn't help but feel his luck was continuing to fail him time and time again, and ever so slowly, Trevor's confidence began to wane.

"I am Trevor Meldew, I am a hard worker, and you should —"

"Sorry, you're not what we're looking for."

"I am Trevor Meldew, I am a hard worker, and you —"

"Are not even remotely interested."

"I am Trevor Meldew, I am a hard worker, and —"

"I'm sure you have a great personality, but we really need a fresh face for our brand, and yours is not."

"I am Trevor Meldew, I am a hard worker —"

"With scrawny arms like those? I think not."

"I am Trevor Meldew, I am a hard —"

"Please, be serious."

"I am Trevor Meldew, I am a —"

"Nope. Next!"

"I am Trevor Meldew, I am —"

"At the wrong table, dear. Now move along."

"I am Trevor Meldew, I —"

"Not if you were the last eligible employee alive."

"I… uh… am Trevor Meldew —"

"Are you sure, you don't sound certain."

"I am Trevor —"

"I'm sorry to hear it, better luck next time."

"I am —"

"That's very philosophical of you, but we're not interested."

"I —"

"I'm sorry, all the positions have been filled by more qualified people."

Leaning against the large mirror in the common room, Trevor felt his tenuous grip on reality begin to loosen. How was it possible he was unemployable? Yes, he was lazy, sure, he didn't maintain the best hygiene standards, he ate way too much junk food, and granted he had a disturbing quality about him that screamed for people to walk in the other direction. But deep down, he was almost certain he was a nice guy.

Looking out at the mass of swirling students, all filling out job applications and shaking hands, and actively avoiding the grocery store table, Trevor couldn't help but feel envious.

Why should they all succeed when he couldn't? It didn't just make him envious, it made him angry! Why should he be punished for his misgivings? *They should all be punished!*

Somewhere in the carefully folded fabric of the unknown universe, there appeared a tiny tear. It's a distinct possibility that the tear occurred thanks to a perfect alignment of various mystical and human elements. A random etching of symbols on a mirror, for example, and the harmonious playing of seven notes ringing through the void of space and time, and also the completely accurate scheduling of a separate job fair taking place in a dark and sinister mirror universe. They all worked in perfect cooperation to create the smallest of tears in the fabric of reality, just big enough for a curly haired, down-on-his-luck moron to slip through.

Trevor fell backwards through the mirror as if it was liquid and tumbled down a small set of stone stairs, landing in an unceremoniously disorganized heap at the bottom. He leapt up and dusted himself off, looking up at the mirror he'd just fallen through. He could still see the job fair happening on the other side of it. It was as if no one had noticed he'd disappeared.

"Wait. Did I just fall through a mirror?"

"Next!" shouted a voice like thirty cats being dragged through a particularly prickly hedge.

Trevor spun around to face the chamber he'd fallen into. It was a vast stone room stretching forever away into darkness. Lava spilled from several holes in the walls and pooled in small stone pockets, throwing a malevolent red glow in the immediate vicinity.

There was also a table before him. A table of dark wood. At the table there sat two people. Although *people* might have been a bit of a stretch.

One was easily eight feet tall, nine if you included the horns. He looked like he was sculpted from rough rock, almost gargoyle-esque, cloven hooves where feet should have been, leathery wings folded neatly at his back, and a long, drawn face with burning red eyes that contained the length and breadth of pain and suffering.

The other looked like a used car salesman with a loud sports jacket, slicked-back hair, and a moustache that walked the fine line between *I grew this to look more manly* and *I own a panel van with no windows and a puppy.*

The less-human-looking creature gestured to the wooden chair on the other side of the table, and against all logic and reasoning, Trevor sat down.

In front of the creature sat a small name card. It read *BOB*. The more human-looking person's card was slightly bigger and read *KLANTAR THE DESTROYER OF TINY THINGS.*

"Glass of water?" asked Bob, whose voice had a soothing quality to it, like fresh coffee being poured first thing in the morning, or Morgan Freeman.

"Or maybe the blood of a tyrant?" said the screechy voice of Klantar the Destroyer of Tiny Things, whose voice when not shouting sounded more like only seventeen cats being dragged through a particularly prickly hedge.

Needless to say, Trevor's day had taken a strange turn.

"So, you're here about the job," said Klantar.

"We're not afraid to admit we've seen a lot of good candidates today," added Bob.

Trevor looked back over his shoulder at the mirrored wall and the students and tables beyond. Wondering briefly if the administrators of the college knew something was wrong with the common-room mirror, he turned back to the two beings before him and did the only logical thing he could.

"I am Trevor Meldew, I am a hard worker, and you should hire me." And then he slid one of his resumes across the table.

Bob snatched it up with a massive clawed hand and perused it.

"See Bob!" Klantar said. "See how easily he lied right there. Like it was second nature."

Bob nodded in agreement, still studying the resume.

"I didn't lie," said Trevor. "That's my name."

Klantar grinned a slimy grin and leaned back in his own chair, clasping both hands behind his head. "Yeah, but you're not a hard worker."

"I am," said Trevor defensively.

"You're not," fired back Klantar.

"Yes, I am," said Trevor, slightly unsure whether this should be the hill he died upon.

"See!" said Klantar again. "It's like second nature to him. He's so confident in his lying, he thinks he's telling the truth."

"But I —"

Klantar leaned forward and slammed his hands down on the table. "Liar!" he shrieked and then laughed a wicked laugh.

Reaching over, Klantar pressed a button on a phone that Trevor had failed to see before. In fact, he was fairly certain it hadn't been there at all.

"Shirley, can you please deliver the file on Trevor Meldew?"

The intercom hissed, a small interdimensional portal *slooshed* open above the table, and a large pink tentacle holding a cardboard banker's box slithered through, depositing the box on the table.

"Thank you, Shirley," said Klantar, and the portal *slooshed* closed.

Bob continued to study the resume, and at one point licked it before saying, "Hmmmmmm."

Klantar threw the lid of the box back over his shoulder and started rifling through papers.

Trevor had the sudden inclination to bolt from the chamber and try and scramble back through the mirror. Maybe he could smash it? Something about the box made him uneasy, like he was suddenly standing naked and every eyeball in the world could see him.

"Alright, age six, you lied to your grandpa about breaking his wooden model boat," said Klantar.

"The cat broke it," said Trevor.

Sloosh! The portal opened again and a single sheet of paper floated through it. Klantar snatched it out of the air and read, "Just now, you again lied about the cat breaking the model boat."

"No, I didn't!" shouted Trevor.

Sloosh! Another piece of paper floated down.

"And now you just lied about lying about the cat breaking the model boat."

Trevor opened his mouth, thought better of it, and closed it again.

Sloosh! Another piece of paper.

"Now you're thinking of trying to lie, but you're worried about everything we know, because it's quickly becoming clear that we do, in fact, know everything about you.

All the bad things Trevor had ever done flashed through his brain.

"Yes," said Klantar, "we know them all."

Trevor wanted to protest, wanted to argue that he wasn't a bad person, but the words wouldn't come out.

"Don't worry," said Klantar. "The fact you're a nefarious lying little underachiever works incredibly in your favour. You're here because you tick all the boxes, my friend."

"What boxes?" asked Trevor, truly curious.

"The boxes for the job. Final decision comes down to my big, evil co-worker here, but I see good things in your future. Well, not good. But definitely things. We need someone like you."

This was a new concept for Trevor. No one ever needed someone like him. They always needed someone distinctly different from him.

"We're always on the lookout for liaisons on earth, you see. Hell doesn't just run because we torture people by poking them with pointy things. Though we do a lot of that too." Klantar laughed hysterically and Bob let out a chuckle.

"A liaison. For Hell?"

"Oh yes, they're everywhere!" said Klantar.

Trevor's mind wandered back to the grocery store recruiter, but Klantar quickly raised his hands.

"Nope, he's not one of ours. Evil? Most certainly. But he's not one of ours. No idea what's wrong with that guy."

"And you want me to be a liaison?"

"You see, we keep a number of offices on earth to make sure things never run smoothly. You've got to throw a bit of chaos in the mix. Keeps all the goodies just a bit off balance." Klantar leaned back again and put both feet up on the table. "You are uniquely qualified."

"I don't think I am," said Trevor. "I've never been qualified for anything."

Klantar snapped forward, slamming his hands down again. "Which makes you perfect! In just the past two weeks, you've exhibited all the traits we love. You're greedy, lazy, unhealthy, angry for no reason, you're prideful, you're a horny little gremlin, and you wish harm would happen to your fellow students because good things don't happen to you. You're our man, Trevor!"

It was nice to be wanted, Trevor couldn't deny it. But this couldn't possibly be right. How could Hell, actual Hell, have offices on earth?

"It's simple!" said Klantar. "We hide in plain sight! Fast food restaurants, greedy companies building spaceships for rich people, lawyers, B-list actors, French EDM artists, Walmart greeters — we're all over the place. We want to place you in a position of power to oversee some of the nasty little things we have in the works. Maybe in time you'll figure out how to engineer an apocalypse. The sky's the limit! What do you say?"

Trevor looked back through the mirror again. *I mean, any job is better than no job.*

"That's the spirit! So, Bob, what do we think? Is Trevor Mildew —"

"Meldew," corrected Trevor.

Klantar waved it off. "Whatever. Is this insignificant, putrid, creature fit to join the team?"

Bob put the resume down carefully, his red eyes ablaze, and placed the tip of a claw on the paper. "Is this Helvetica Neue Ultralight *Italic*?"

Trevor nodded.

Bob stared at him for so long that Trevor began to feel the weight of tortured souls clawing at the back of his brain, and for a brief moment he began to regret his font choice.

"This," said Bob, "is the most evil of all the fonts. You're perfect, you're hired, welcome to Hell Incorporated."

With that, he flapped his wings and flew off into the darkness.

"Congratulations, kid!" said Klantar. "We'll send you a uniform and get you to work. Shirley! Show Mopdrew out."

"Meldew," said Trevor, but Klantar had already disappeared.

Sloosh! The portal popped open and Shirley's tentacle shot out, wrapped itself around Trevor, and thrust him back toward the mirrored wall. Trevor screamed such a shrill scream that, despite the interdimensional separation of it all, the grocery store recruiter briefly thought he might have heard something. The mirrored wall rushed toward him, Trevor braced for impact and then *SLOOSH!*

He woke up in bed.

Conveniently, it was his own bed.

In his dorm room.

The sun shone through the window.

He was wearing pyjamas.

What the hell just happened?

Checking the date on his phone, it was the 23rd. The day after the job fair. Had he gone to the job fair? Did he party too hard and miss an entire day? What kind of a crazy dream was that?

None of that could have actually happened. He must have been blackout drunk, it was the only explanation. The day lay before him and he could buckle down and get some homework done, maybe go and hand out some resumes as he'd clearly missed the job fair. He would, he'd do it! He'd make something of himself.

Or… he could just throw on some clothes and go steal some food from one of his dorm mates and veg out for the day. Yes, that sounded like a better idea.

Rolling out of bed, Trevor failed to notice the red tie hanging off his mirror. He also didn't notice the coffee stain, because Trevor was lazy like that. He didn't notice the stack of brownish resumes on the desk or the fact the edges of the paper were slightly burned.

As he walked away from his reflection, he completely failed to see the new set of horns and the tail his reflection was now sporting.

Trevor stepped out into the dorm hallway, comfortably wrapped in the blind ignorance that he was about to unleash his very own brand of chaos upon the world.

WEST OF **ALBERTA**

HARRISON KIM

Spencer fidgeted in the bus depot waiting room, waiting on a transfer. He had an hour until departure, and he knew what to do from here on.

"The rules are clear," he thought. "Walk on the red light. Go on the green. Be sociable and polite. Pay for your tickets and stay in the line. Hell, I've been a good boy."

So why was he still feeling so pissed off?

Spencer watched his wife, Kayla, sitting in the depot café across from him. She chewed gum behind the plexiglass that separated the waiting room from the dining area. She masticated up and down, back and forth, as if she had all day.

Spencer wanted to crunch his suitcase into that plexiglass.

"What the hell is going on with her?" he muttered.

He remembered the long bus ride. No movement for hours, sitting in the steel bus shell while the world rolled by. His wife quiet, always quiet. She liked things the same. Watching TV and smoking cigarettes. Not even looking out the window at the mountains. Always staring straight ahead at the next bus seat. Didn't she know that change was good, mountains were beautiful? Spencer had changed. He was sober now. Sober for the last two weeks. Couldn't Kayla understand that?

"She can't accept reality," Spencer thought. "We're going to a new home. A new city. We're going to start a new life."

He felt calmer now. He turned his head, viewed other people in the bus depot. Their faces resembled animal faces. Here, a jackass pacing. There, a cockroach scuttling. In the line-up, sheep. The restaurant: pigs. What kept them alive? Only the heartbeat to reach tomorrow? There were projects to build, ideas to explore, music and nature. If you sat around, you might as well be slaughtered. Spencer was different from them. He'd never be ground up and cast aside. He had values, self-regulation. He wasn't on the wagon of buying and selling and competing, like the scrabbling mob. He was different.

"Yeah, different," he repeated to himself. "I stopped drinking, just did it. Pure willpower."

Spencer glanced over at the café to observe a strange person sitting with his wife. The back of a head. Long black hair, sloping shoulders. Hands passing his wife a coffee cup. Kayla smiling.

"What makes her smile like that?" Spencer wondered. "What's so goddamn funny?"

He walked up to the plexiglass border and hit it with the end of his suitcase. The stranger turned around. Spencer saw a scraggly black beard, big eyes highlighted by mascara. Kayla stopped smiling. Spencer marched into the restaurant, swinging his suitcase.

"Who the hell are you?" he demanded.

"A friend," said the stranger. A stranger with a deep voice, but from under a purple, sleeveless muscle shirt poked what resembled women's breasts with fat nipples. A stranger with narrow pointy teeth and long, dark arm hair. A stranger wearing red lipstick and throat rings pierced beneath a large Adam's apple. Some kind of bus depot mutant.

"How long have you been drinking together?" Spencer banged his suitcase near his wife's knee.

Kayla lifted her coffee and smiled, as if he'd told a joke.

"I'm stone cold sober," she said. "After all, it's only my first cup."

She giggled, and the stranger smiled back.

"Why don't you join us?" The stranger rubbed their beard hairs. "I'm not with her, we're merely having a conversation."

"You're with her, all right," said Spencer. "Dragging her into your world."

The stranger sat back. "You were the one who barged in here," he said.

Spencer reached down and grabbed his wife's arm.

"Let's go. The bus is leaving pronto."

"Hey." His wife shook herself away. She slapped at the back of Spencer's hand. "I want to finish my coffee."

Spencer jumped back. There she was, defiant in a public place. Anything to make a scene. And she'd hit him. Her face below his, long, hairless, and shiny. Hair brown, curly, bunched up on one side. She hadn't combed it since they arrived.

"I'm not trying to tempt you or anything," said the stranger, "but there's lots of time for a second cup."

He blinked big eyes and opened a small bottle, poured some of the contents into his coffee. Kayla nodded, and the stranger nodded too, lifting his head to look at Spencer.

"I'm completely harmless," the stranger said. "Don't make a mountain out of a finger bowl."

"I decide what's real around here!" Spencer shouted. "What the hell are you pouring into that cup?"

Other customers looked up from various tables.

Spencer grabbed the back of his wife's neck and pulled. She tossed her coffee on the floor, cried, "For Christ's sake!" but did not resist his pull, rose with the force of his lifting fingertips.

"Okay, okay," she said.

A customer brandished his fork, shook it in Spencer's direction.

The counterperson leaned over her counter.

"You stop that, mister! I'll call security."

"It's our business," said Spencer.

His wife's face stiffened. She looked up at him.

"But I want it," she said. "Just another cup of coffee."

"Look what you've done," said the stranger. "You've made her cry."

"Mind your fucking business," Spencer said.

The stranger shrugged. "You could have joined us."

Spencer crowded his wife into the waiting room. He pulled her down hard on a stained brown bench.

"I'm sorry," he said, "but you've got to follow the rules. Stop at red lights. Smoke in the right section. Don't talk to weird people, like that guy. It's an evil world out there. Anything can happen."

As he talked, he felt dizzy, the bus depot reeling slowly around him, his jaw tight, clenched. He clutched his suitcase to his side, pulled his other arm over his wife. She moved away, he shuffled closer. Their legs touched. She stared straight ahead.

"I didn't even get a chance to drink my coffee," she said. She leaned forward to put two dollars in the television machine. "I never get a chance."

"Who was that freak of nature you were sitting with?" Spencer asked. "Was it trying to pick you up?"

He held her closer.

"Just a passing acquaintance," she said. "A friendly face."

She squeezed out of Spencer's grip and moved to the end of the bench.

"Please don't," Spencer said. "Please don't go with strangers. Didn't you see his booze flask?"

"I just wanted another cup," she said, grabbing for her purse.

Spencer stared at her. Skinny neck, red-rimmed eyes, stupid faux fur coat all askew. And as he kept looking, the waiting room stopped reeling. As he smelled her breath of coffee and whiskey, it calmed him. He gazed at her unlaced, knee-high boots, and the sight of skinny, black-stockinged legs coming out their tops steadied his mind.

He surveyed the waiting room. This could be the whole world, laid out in tableau, as he struggled forward with this journey, to build a new existence. The pigs, sheep, and cockroach people waited to ruin his plans and cast him down to their level. But the rules supported his stability, gave him structure. Told him right from wrong, kept him from falling. Stick to the laws, and all would be well. Seek order through the chaos, and light through the darkness. Love thy neighbour as thyself. Wait your turn to buy a ticket. Don't give in to temptation. Exercise willpower.

"The bus will arrive soon," he said.

Kayla sighed. "If we're lucky," she replied.

The stranger with the beard and makeup waved from the café behind the plexiglass.

Kayla tried to tie up her boots and wave back at the same time. She pointed at a security guard, who'd appeared in the foyer. The guard looked around, then fixed his eyes on Spencer and his wife.

"There's nothing wrong with me," Kayla said. "The world is changing, Spencer. You're not gonna be pushing me around all the time."

As she spoke, Spencer felt his rage return at the whiny sound of her voice, and behind this rage, a growing helplessness, because he knew there was absolutely nothing he could do to stop himself. He would break free from the rules, toss all limits, and lose everything.

FIRST PLACE — **FICTION**

I loved so many things about this story. The characterization that kicks in right from the start with the knowledge that we are in the hands of an alcoholic, and so a very unreliable narrator. The hallucinatory imagery caused by his withdrawal. Spencer's certainty that he is absolutely in the right in what he observes and how he behaves. The strangeness of some of the language reflecting the themes. Loved the phrase above: "Don't make a mountain out of a finger bowl." There's a jaggedness to the writing style, which enhances the content. It's unsettling, as if the reader is in the station café, observing this man and woman, wondering if it's all going to escalate. Edgy and very skilfully done.

— Chris (C.C.) Humphreys

Finding **Joy**

Serena Caner

"Mzungu! Mzungu!" The voices of children sing as they dance, following me like the Pied Piper. *Mzungu. White Person.* I walk awkwardly, not used to the attention or the chitenje wrapped around my waist, glad when someone shoos them away. I have come to the place where bougainvillea no longer billow over barbed wire fences and jacaranda cease to shelter quiet roads. Where the pavement ends and the dirt begins — this is Kauma village. More of an informal settlement than village, thirty thousand Malawians have migrated here seeking employment and opportunity, but their reality is bleak — subsistence farmers without land to cultivate; youth without elders to educate; disease without doctors to mitigate. They speak Chichewa, Chilomwe, Chiyao, Chingoni, Chitumbuka, but need English to find a job.

"Come Selina, this way to my home!"

He smiles at me, and it hurts, knowing what I have done. We pass rows of rundown mud bungalows without toilets, power, or running water, and his reality sinks in, filling my eyes with tears.

"Do not cry," he says. "God is good. He will find a way." I wish I had his faith in God or humanity, but it has been shattered. I came to Malawi on an internship to help people, but my good intentions are not enough.

This is a valuable lesson for you to learn on these internships. As a foreigner, you must understand that there is a cultural dynamic that you cannot readily identify. After a year of working with Malawians, I am keenly aware of this dynamic. I know the importance of determining what level of salary paid to local workers is "fair." Salary scales depend on the level of local economies, and these, in turn depend on global economics. We checked around to figure out what a fair salary would be for security and we knew that we were being generous.

The crow of the rooster outside my window is startling, but I am already awake, having spent the night listening to every new sound, imagined or real — the mosquitoes hovering outside my netting; cockroaches scurrying across the floor; the distant yelping of a dog fight. The events of the previous days replay in my mind — my advocacy had unintentionally resulted in the security guard's dismissal. They made no plea for mercy, only turned and left, their shoulders sagging to the floor. And then, in an act of solidarity, or perhaps seeking atonement, the decision to move to their village. I kick off my sleeping bag and cross the compound yard to the outhouse where a mangy dog sleeps. He jumps up, flies swarming on his festering wound, and it occurs to me that if I got rabies, it would be exactly what I deserved.

It is well beyond our capacity to change a global economic system. I would hope that what you have experienced today will motivate you to find out just how it is that we (in Canada) are so monetarily rich, and they are so poor. Unfortunately, there is great unfairness in the world.

The village well is a meeting place for women. Besides water, they pump gossip, and rumours of the foreigner have leaked. They stare at me with a mix of curiosity and pity, noting my white sneakers, covered with clay and shame. One woman calls over and they all start to giggle.

"Mzungu, muli bwanji!"

My cheeks turn shiny and red, like my new plastic bucket, and I am tongue-tied until they resume their morning ritual — filling and lifting buckets of water onto their heads. They don't spill a drop, either on themselves or the babies sleeping on their backs. They depart as a group, elegant as gazelles, but despite their heavy loads, they stop to shake my hand and welcome me. I wait until they are out of sight before I attempt to fill my own bucket, barely able to lift it off the ground. I hold it like a *mzungu*, by the handle, and with each step, water splashes over the sides as it thumps painfully against my shin. When my fingers lose circulation, I put it down, noticing the boy watching me. His shirt is threadbare, a veil over his skin, but I can tell by his expression that his mind is grappling with a much more profound question — *how do they carry water in your country?* Our eyes meet and he points to the top of his head, as if to tell me, *"It's easy; just put it on your head!"* For a moment, I can visualize myself lifting the bucket up, balancing it carefully as I walk. I bend over, sizing it up, gripping the rim. The boy, as if foreseeing the disaster, runs over to help. He takes one side of the bucket and we raise it up towards my shoulders, until he can no longer reach. Without his help, my arms begin to wobble and the water tips all over me. He hides his laughter until he realizes I am also laughing, keeled over, at our existential predicaments — a boy, living in a world that cannot grace him with a shirt, and a woman, who cannot carry her own pail of water.

Other people cannot continue paying salaries to guards that are well above the local standard after we are gone. That would be unsustainable. That is what we mean by "sustainability of interventions." While money is an issue (the power to acquire material goods), if we simply "throw money" at people without finding ways whereby THEY THEMSELVES can sustain their lives, I pose to you that we are simply being "charitable" and we are not contributing to people's development.

When I get back to my hut, an act of kindness waits on my doorstep — a bucket full of water. Looking around, I see the boy hiding behind a woman's skirt. She extends her hand.

"*Muli bwanji.* My name is Doris. You are most welcome."

"You speak English," I say, relieved.

"Yes, I am a teacher. Don't worry, you will learn Chichewa. *Pang'ono, pang'ono, bas.*"

I point to the bucket on my porch, scrap pieces of aluminum welded together.

"Thank you for the water. I spilled mine earlier."

"In Malawi, we have a saying: *Pendapenda sikugwa koma kuchalira ulendo.* Stumbling is not falling, but getting ready for the journey."

"That's a nice way to put it. In my country, they would call me clumsy."

"*Aaah-Sah,*" she says, recognizing my humour, "we will learn much from each other." She pulls the boy out from behind her. "This one is Chimwemwe, my sister's firstborn. Anything you need, he will help you."

"Can you say his name again?"

"Chimwemwe. It means 'joy.' "

I bend over, holding out my hand.

"*Muli bwanji*, Chimwemwe."

His face lights up and he flashes pearly white teeth. Then he runs off, returning with a broom made of tied-up branches and begins to sweep the dirt outside my hut. Doris whispers, "He is an orphan; my sister passed away from malaria."

Our project only has funding until March. We are looking for further funding, but the reality is that if we do not find this funding, we are all out of a job, and the only people who will suffer are the Malawians.

A couple of months pass and it is time to say goodbye. I throw a party, purchasing live chickens from the market that give their final squawk before we slit their throats and pluck their feathers. I try to explain to Doris that I have never killed a chicken before, because in Canada, it appears magically cleaned and cut up in the store. Doris clucks her teeth, passing handfuls of its stringy intestines over to gathering children. They slurp them up like noodles, shrieking with glee. While the chicken is frying, I begin my most important task — cooking the daily sustenance, *nsima*. With a pot balancing on three stones over a fire, I stir the freshly ground maize flour into water, until it is thick and bubbly. The smoke from the fire hovers in the cook shack, making my eyes water, but I keep going, knowing that I am cooking for a crowd. Beads of sweat line my brow as I beat the mixture stiff, my wooden paddle thwacking rhythmically against the sides of the pot.

"You are a Malawian now," Doris says, her face beaming with pride. As we eat under the light of the moon, it occurs to me that I am surrounded by some of the richest and most joyful people in the world. My heart aches, knowing that without a formal address or Internet, I may never hear from them again. I spot Chimwemwe, sitting beside a bucket of water. It is a child-sized bucket, but I walk over, lifting it onto my head, all on my own. He claps and I try to curtsy, until the water spills all over me again.

HONOURABLE MENTION — **NONFICTION**

This is a skilful call and response between contractual language and the reality the writer experiences in a temporary internship in Malawi. A few well-chosen moments highlighting life in a settlement of economic migrants, some passages from documents outlining the difficulties of ensuring ongoing funding to maintain an assistance programme: these serve to immerse the reader in a complicated situation.

— Theresa Kishkan

It's **Okay** for People **to Be Angry**

Melissa Sawatsky

Sometimes, I turn away from the
newsreels, social feeds, catastrophes, tragedies
and then it turns inward.

A nonspecific anger at
my spouse, the town in which I live,
my daughter
my *self*.

Fingernails press, then
puncture my palm. I punch
my fist on the arm of the rocking chair,
relish the throb. Taste blood on my tongue.

My two-year-old screams into the centre of my eardrums
and it's okay. She is feeling
her feelings. They are big. It's okay
for her to be big with anger.

She has taken note of her size.
She is small compared to me;
I am small compared to Daddy. She pushes against
this heteronormative, patriarchal, generational
hierarchy.

Scream, baby.

HONOURABLE MENTION — **POETRY**

*The poem here is very raw, exposed, real, and shares such inti-
mate moments of one understanding their place and how they
can tear away at that. Thinking of concepts like anger and what
that truly means for a person, and how we are brought into a
space that no one wants to be through different methods, and that
that's sometimes okay too. The poem speaks to the condition of the
human body and how fragile we all really are, and how we just
need someone to care for us. But it comes back to the sense that
it's all okay, we can admit when we need assistance, we can admit
when we need help.*

— Conor Kerr

The Buoyancy of Running Shoes

Caitlin Hicks

They found another human foot near Westham Island in Ladner. This one, discovered by a couple while walking their dog, was a lefty. That morning, before the shooting of that young man, before Claire, I'd read it in the papers over cappuccino at the Tate.

Five disarticulated feet had washed up on the shores of beach islands in the BC archipelago since 2007, and each time another foot was found, I'd trolled the web for lurid details. From my home office in London's NW3 neighbourhood, after I had concluded a day's work, I would sit at my computer, looking out onto the narrow, cobbled drive to the apartment building across the street, and discovered such things as: each foot was wearing a sneaker, two were size 12, only one was a woman's foot.

I learned about the buoyancy of running shoes before the girls came home from kindergarten, and found the Facebook site for two hundred missing men from the lower mainland (whose DNA were being compared with the missing feet). After we took Polly for a walk, after supper, after we read *One Fish Two Fish Red Fish Blue Fish* and concluded our bedtime rituals, I considered the theories: discarded bodies left over from organ harvesting; a serial killer; a weirdo working at a funeral parlour (who looks at feet when paying respects?).

Perhaps I was more than casually interested in the specific assortment of human remains, because they had turned up in a corner of the world I had fled when my wife died — the west coast of British Columbia, abundant in sea and sky, forest and wild, a place whose skies are either raining, about to rain, or have just emptied themselves of rain.

For a long time, I didn't connect the feet to anything — certainly not to the night I lost her, and yet, with the feet, as with my wife's death, here was something intrinsically magnetic and repulsive, and as much as I tried to look away, I couldn't.

To my own surprise, the two hundred missing men had lured me into stories about suicides off the Golden Gate Bridge, where the seventy-nine metre fall (two hundred and twenty-three feet) takes only four seconds, and jumpers hit the water between seventy-five and eighty-eight miles per hour. I tried to imagine jumping into the twelve-storey void, shattering my spine, having my internal organs ripped from their moorings, and then drowning in the forty-seven-degree water, but I couldn't quite imagine the despair required to do it. Massive currents beneath the bridge wash many jumpers into oblivion, or great white sharks finish them off in the bay. Only one person is said to have jumped without injury — in 1985, a sixteen-year-old wrestler landed on his butt and swam ashore; his first words, "I can't do anything right."

Normally, a body sinks, fills with gas, and bobs to the surface of the water. Normally head, feet and hands can detach after submersion, but they don't usually float. So, how were the feet being washed up on beaches? Each new discovery revealed another detail that led to another mystery. The sea turns some submerged body parts (especially feet) into a soap-like substance called adipocere, which preserves them. If a load of sneakers gets dumped into the sea, certain currents would carry only right shoes and other currents, only left.

The ocean sorts things out to an exquisite degree.

Eight other feet had shown up on the beaches of California, Ottawa, Spain, New Zealand, and Britain since 2004. Could there be enough in the speculation surrounding the feet to warrant the making of a film? 'Research' had been my excuse to indulge in the obsessive trailings after every scrap of gruesome detail — even though I was then editing-for-hire and would probably not venture into independent filmmaking again, the way things were going.

Bridges could be my middle name. But it's Gabriel, after my grandfather, who designed and built bridges, the most famous being the McClugage Bridge over Upper Peoria Lake in Illinois. I thought this heritage was the reason I have been plagued with nightmares about bridges, and possibly why I was now so curious about the missing feet. Ever since I was a child, in my recurring nightmare, I am looking down at roaring white water through a steel grate as my stomach lurches towards the rapids. Or I have to cross a rickety creaker made of balsa wood stretched over a canyon, with a stream up the middle so thin and far away, it looks like a line drawn on a map. Or, it's a rope — on fire — and I have cross a canyon on it.

The truth was, except for the sporadic nightmares about being on a bridge, the stories inherent in the discovery of another found foot touched me only a little, but I savoured each small titillation. Even my curiosity about them was a curiosity to me. It had been a long time since anything had caught my emotional attention. My recent obsession with the feet was more feeling than I'd had about anything since the first night — almost five years ago — when the twins and I closed the door behind us and found ourselves alone together, in London.

By the time the missing feet were found — the morning of the Tate Incident, there was nothing left of Lisa. I had scattered her ashes in the waters of Georgia Strait before the long plane flight with the baby girls — but now, five years later, I found myself imagining the light in the water as what was left of her became part of the ocean floor under someone's foot still in its shoe.

It was a sensationally ordinary July afternoon, and of course, none of us were expecting anything to happen, certainly not something life-altering. I was reading a letter from an old friend.

"Dear Timothy, July 10, 2008

"I can't even remember how long it's been. A long time. Bernadette and Maddie must be quite tall by now. Their photo on my refrigerator is greasy and smudged — and they're just little lumps in two bundles in my arms. You could be married for all I know. I have news."

We were, all three of us — me and the girls — sitting in a noisy café in London's New Tate Gallery. It was a humid, overcast day; we sat at a booth, picking at our wilted lunch as the room teemed with tourists.

Bernadette squirmed in the seat next to me, her knobby knees peeking out from a lightweight yellow frock we'd just gotten back from the laundry — so far, no dribbles. She was trying to decipher our letter from her brother, Max, where he had printed a message for her at the bottom in big felt-tip letters. Salty crisps rested on a green plate greasy with fingerprints.

"Low — vuh." She slowly mouthed sounds indicated by the letters on the page.

"How does the baby get out?" Maddie pestered, pointing to a woman in the queue. I turned my head towards the line-up and saw the huge belly of a pregnant woman. Fertility hung on her like the ripe weight of fresh fruit, her plump face flushed and glowing in the heat. I found myself watching her voluptuous breasts moving up and down with her breathing.

"Dad?" Maddie pulled on my arm. "Her tummy looks eeeeeNORmous!"

"The mother's stomach opens up when the sun shines on it," Bernadette quipped authoritatively, looking up from her letter. I glanced back at mine.

"Your tenants are expecting a baby and have moved quite abruptly to Powell River, so as of today your house is empty. I can hardly believe it's been five years already since the twins were born and you left! Anyway, haven't you had enough of London yet?"

"Do you think she has twins in there?"

"It sure looks like there could be."

"Did our mother look like that?"

"She was pretty big."

I couldn't concentrate. In his note to us, Max had complained about how he still hadn't found his birth mother. I was helpless in the face of his frustration; I knew his birth father, but the mother's identity had been a deliberate secret from the moment Lisa and I agreed to take him as our own. Adding to the undertow of anxiety, in the news, London police had stumbled onto a terrorist cell, averting a disaster skedded for the weekend (this being the Saturday).

"Of course, I will have the place re-rented under our agreement if you aren't ready to return. Better would be that you face your demons — and your friends — and come back here! With

the state of the world these days, Canada is still a good place to be.

"I'm sure you have a girlfriend or a wife, you're too cute to be on your own for long. Bring her too, but let me know what you plan to do. — Teresa"

"Daaad!"

I glanced at Maddie. She had snatched and wolfed back the cylindrical biscuit on the saucer of my cappuccino, and little bits were left at the corners of her mouth. Lately, the twins had become insatiable for details about their mother.

"What did Max have to say, Bernadette?" I asked, pointing to her brother's letter in her hand. Practiced diversionary tactic on my part.

"Tell us again about Mom when we were born," Maddie continued, much too smart to let the topic die unexplored. Bernadette, however, suddenly saw meaning in the words printed at the bottom of her letter.

"'I love you!'" she exclaimed, her face infused with pride.

"I love you!" Maddie spontaneously reached for her sister — through the obstacle of my stomach.

"Listen," I said.

In the distance, we heard anxious shouting voices and the sound of hard shoes stepping quickly over marble floors.

A gangly young man came charging towards us, dispersing a queue of heat-fatigued tourists in shorts staring at the blue Klein painting in the room at the end of the hall. A swirl of startled mumbling gathered around the group like buzzing bees as he sprinted through them.

He rounded the corner into the café and pulled on the purse straps of the pregnant woman, skidding to a stop with her as his anchor. Her bag slid forward onto her huge belly, and he shook it off his hand, releasing it back to her. He turned his head right and left, casting wildly about for an opening, then leapt over the glass separator towards the kitchen. He hopped into the steaming silver trays of mashed potatoes, past stunned employees with large utensils in their hands, disappearing into the kitchen.

The pregnant woman now seemed to occupy the middle of the room, framed by light. Skinny ostrich legs propped up her enormous girth. Four men burst into the café, handguns drawn. Rounding the corner, they too had trouble stopping short of pushing the girl over, their heads looking quickly right, then left. Everyone else scrambled to the floor, as hurried conversation quieted to an eerie silence. Still standing, as if in a trance, the woman held her belly, an island of calm.

Maybe this is the terrorist thing they supposedly averted.

Our table was about twelve feet away and looked out onto the open space the woman now occupied solo. My arms stiffened around Maddie and Bernadette and I pulled their faces onto my lap on either side of me under the table. The men pushed through an opening on the far side into the kitchen. Pots and pans clanged, and a firecracker sound exploded in that room, a gunshot probably. Screaming. My first thought was to get out of the café but *best not to be a moving target.*

The pregnant woman stood as if frozen in her tracks. I looked at my girls. Their eyes poured all their fear and trust into mine. I was glued to the spot, my body coursing with an irresistible instinct to hover over them, shielding them with my own girth. I glanced at Bernadette and back at the pregnant woman, feeling the familiar reluctance to speak to someone I don't know. Another shot in the kitchen and something inside of me broke open. The girls would be fine if they kept under the table. The woman was in danger of being shot.

"Stay here. Don't move." Bernadette's gaze darted from one of my eyes to the other, looking for any wavering in my resolve.

I looked into Maddie's eyes, she nodded confidently — we were in collusion. I pulled away from them, moving towards the standing woman.

"I think you should get down," I said to reassure her as I put my arms around her wide girth from behind. It took a few seconds but she understood what I was doing and both of us struggled to the floor together.

In that instant, I remembered Lisa on a hospital bed with the sides up, my arms around her big belly. Lightly, I'd stroked my knuckles across her back and the warmth at the base of her spine had leapt onto the back of my hand.

Lisa, I'd said, *I have a feeling about this.*

Stay with me, she whispered. *Whatever happens.*

My nose practically touched the translucent skin of the woman's shoulder. Her damp smell — sweat, musk, and something metallic and sweet — permeated the air. Wisps of her black hair clung to the nape of her neck.

"*Daddy!*" Bernadette's whining voice. If I looked back, she would run to me.

"Let's get under the counter," I said, pushing the back of the young woman's knees with mine. We heard a shot, dishes breaking, screaming. Someone leapt over the food and back into the café, landing in front of us. The young man. I pushed myself a few inches back from the mother-to-be and lifted my head: I could see blood on the floor. And his face.

Such a face, so much like my own son, waken from a bad dream, pleading terror in his brown eyes, as if he was going to say *Daddy* at any second.

"Daddy!" Bernadette screamed.

I strained around to see Bernadette pulling towards me as Maddie held her back by the arm.

"Get *down*, Bernadette!" I yelled across the room.

The young man struggled to push himself off the floor and staggered into the Klein room, a trail of blood dripping onto the marble floor. His assailants leapt over the potatoes in pursuit; as they stepped past us I moved my foot, tripping one of them. *They're not going to get that boy; they're so wrong about him.* I had looked into his eyes and I knew: he was not the man they were looking for. He was just a boy, for some reason, running for his life.

The officer on the ground rolled over towards me, realizing something had tripped him. His face was taut with pent up desperation. He lifted his gun. I stared him down for a long moment. The room quieted, except for the whirr of the refrigerators as we held our collective breath. The hot metallic smell of blood filled my nostrils. I tilted my head towards the woman so obviously fat with child.

"We're just trying to get out of the way."

He hesitated, held me in his gaze. Then Bernadette shrieked from across the room.

"Daddy!"

I lowered my voice, as calm as I could manage. "Honey, stay there. Please. Just stay where you are."

The officer glanced over his shoulder at Maddie and Bernadette; recognition flickered in his eyes. He pushed himself up off the floor and scrambled out the door.

We heard the sound of shoes chasing over the marble floors, up the stairs and into the distance. Sirens wailing louder, then fading.

Little arms around my neck — Madeline hugged me from behind; Bernadette fit herself into the space between the woman's back and my stomach. All our hearts beat the same, a frightened, grateful beat — together.

We clambered up together and I put my hand out to help this woman off the floor. The room began to awaken into disbelief, into sobs and chatter.

"Is that real blood, Daddy?" Maddie leaned over and put her forefinger into the puddle of blood on the floor, retracting it like she was pushing a button, then wiping her finger onto her frock.

"Maddie!" I yelled, grabbing her hand and examining her forefinger in a futile gesture. The woman faced away from us rather ungracefully on all fours, trying to push up to standing. I held her elbow, bent my knees to support the weight of her body struggling against mine. As she righted herself, she looked calmly into my eyes for a second — hers were green and speckled. A gush of warm water splashed all of us and shot out onto the floor, mingling with the blood. Bernadette burst into tears; I grabbed her up onto my hip as she sobbed inconsolably into my shoulder.

There was a lot of water. Maddie stomped her foot into the expanding puddle, spraying us, giggling.

"Maddie, *stop* it!"

"So sorry," the woman said. "I think my water's just broken." A couple of security guards came towards the café with their arms outstretched.

"Ladies and gentlemen, please remain calm. We'd like to retain you for questioning." They stood at the edges of the café near the door, as if to corral us there. The woman, still quite self-possessed, reached her hand towards me.

"I'm Claire," she said, shaking my hand. "My labour's progressing. It's going well, but I just can't stay." Maddie grabbed a hold of my jacket. I looked at her and shrugged, watching Claire walk past the lunch counter.

"Can I phone someone for you? Your husband?" I offered, trailing her resolute gait. "I have a mobile." The kitchen stood silent, an empty witness. A huge iron pot on the stove billowed the misty steam of a rolling boil. Several plates of food sat under yellow lights; others on a stainless steel counter waited, half filled. Below my feet, a trail of blood scuffed the cement floor. The door swung behind us.

"Once we get out of here, you can phone my midwife." She called over her shoulder.

Great, I thought, we'll get her on her way. I was thoroughly shaken; could feel something inside me blurring; wanted to hold up for the girls. The swinging door behind me flapped. A bobby — the white shirt and vest, the checkerboard stripe across the hat, navy trousers, baton.

"You can't be going," he announced.

Shit, I thought. *How many hours of British inefficiency are we going to have to endure here? This morning, there was a three-hour delay in the underground because of… leaves ? On the track?* Mentally I began to launch — there is so much incompetence to complain about here in London, and I had spent hours frustrated on the helpless end of each. Claire turned around. She slumped next to the stainless steel counter, holding her belly. I dropped Bernadette to her feet and caught Claire before she hit the floor. For some reason, I remembered that a bobby doesn't wear a gun.

"This is an emergency," I said with an urgency that surprised me. "This woman is going to deliver any second, and we don't want her bleeding to death!" My voice was thin and panicked. "We have to get out of here." Claire righted herself again, full of her original self-possession.

"I'm not going to bleed to death," she said, grinning, as if she had already looked into the glass ball of her future and it had predicted she'd win the lottery. *Jeez, that was knee-jerk! Calm, Timothy!* The bobby stood stock still, looking confused and frightened, yet determined to have his questions answered. I grabbed Claire's hand, squeezed it, hard. She looked up to my face. I gestured, rolling my eyes towards the bobby. She collapsed against me again.

"Get me an escort," I barked. "Royal Free Hospital, Hampstead."

"We can go out the back," the bobby replied, shaken.

"They have a 17 per cent caesarean rate," she whispered to me.

"It's the only one I know of," I told her. "The girls were there one night for a fever."

"I'm registered at Edgeware Birth Centre."

A few blocks away, legs circling, arms flailing, the young man tumbled into the Thames from Millennium Bridge. Gravity carried him into the churning waters: he had climbed up the steel cables over the railing and leapt into the air.

At twelve thirty the next morning, the phone rang next to my bed. I was wide awake.

"It's a boy!" Claire chirped excitedly. "And it all went so well, except that he was crying a bit at the start. I don't know what he could possibly be complaining about."

"Congratulations," I offered. It's great they have those one-word replies for situations like these; I rely on them.

"He's so beautiful, he's right here, can you hear him?" Some rustling sounds, like she was putting the receiver to his mouth.

I had to admit I couldn't hear anything

"Quiet, idn't he?" She laughed, as if she were playing a joke on me. "His name is Eamon, do you like it?" She didn't wait for my reply. "Listen, before I go on any more, I have to tell you, the girls are asleep, probably, but tell them, so neither of them ever forget the night that this baby boy came into the world, and the nice man who helped, I named him Eamon Timothy Hale. After you."

"Well, right, Timothy *is* my name. Actually, it's not a bad name," I added, immediately regretting my gaffe. "You didn't have to."

"No, I did. You stepped right up in the café, and we're both probably alive because of it. I was in labour and I could only concentrate on one thing at a time."

As the girls thrashed and murmured on either side of me, Claire chattered ecstatically for a half an hour, and would have probably gone on if Maddie hadn't wet the bed.

I was only able to fall asleep after 5:00 a.m., once I had made my decision.

I woke much later, to the sound of Lisa's breath in my ear, the scent of her smell lingering on the sheets.

This story, under a slightly different name ("Disarticulated"), won first place for fiction in the Beachcombers 50th Anniversary Literary and Art Contest, sponsored by the Sunshine Coast Writers and Editors Society in 2022.

TROUVAILLE: A LEGACY FOR GENERATIONS

DONNA VANSANT

As we drive the rough back roads of the old Douglas Ranch Trail, the smell of winter blows crisply across the lake. It is late fall in the Nicola Valley and a few members of the Pennask Lake Fishing and Game Club gather for the last catch of the season. That evening, we enjoy the usual five-star dining experience and end the meal with a fresh apple tarte Tatin. The fruit is picked from the old apple trees which dot the landscape. These trees, reminiscent of Johnny Appleseed, prevail, leaving a legacy of the past apple orchards. The trees, for the most part, are now replaced by vineyards heralding the Okanagan wine industry. The apple taste, a lingering paradox of past and present.

I sit back and think that James Dole, the well-known Pineapple King, would be happy knowing that this Kentucky/Calgary girl is thoroughly enjoying his legacy — the lodge, the anticipated catch, the meals and the collegial milieu between the American and Canadian membership. Historical records indicate that James travelled to British Columbia and felt a deep connection to the pristine backcountry, and by chance, discovered rainbow trout. So captured by the spectacular fishing adventure, James bought twenty-five-hundred acres around Pennask Lake, including sixteen of the twenty-five kilometres of lakeshore. He started a fishing club and built a lodge so that he and his friends could visit Canada and enjoy the fly fishing. To this day, the lure of the catch keeps us coming back year after year.

On the wall of the lobby is a framed certificate verifying that the royal family, Queen Elizabeth and Prince Philip, officially visited the lodge in 1959. When you invite your guests to fly fish at Pennask, you always regale them with the fact that the Queen once graced this very lodge. The royal visit is a historical marker of pride for the membership. I lean forward as I listen carefully to the rumours about this visit. I am actually eavesdropping. Little do I know that during the next few hours, I will discover the truth about the Queen's night flight.

My imagination travels to that time, the late '50s in British Columbia — deep-gouged back roads, ranch country, and rolling hills full of hearsay gold. I also feel the drumming of the *Battle of New Orleans* and Johnny Horton's popular refrain, "We fired our guns and the British kept a-coming." What could be more British than the royal family visiting Pennask Lodge, deep in the woods of Gold Country?

Pennask Lodge itself is old and rustic — tucked on the lakeshore and nestled among the loons who continually taunt and pester the fishers. Built in 1930, its bedrooms are on the second and third floor with mostly twin beds, shared bathrooms and showers, and steep stairways challenging the elderly clientele. Its patrons, used to luxurious comfort, relish in the nostalgic idea of roughing it in nature. To be sure, it is splendid isolation, and we always catch fish! Beautiful rainbow trout.

That evening, guests leisurely scatter in the lodge — full and satiated, some enjoy the fireplace ambience in the lounge, others settle in the "loon's nest" playing Trivial Pursuit and indulging in after-dinner drinks, and still others begin to get ready for bed as fishing starts early next morning. That night, it is serene and almost too quiet. The moon, barely visible, is covered by whispering fog. The cold looming. It feels eerie.

Yikes. I spill red wine and normally don't even drink red wine! It dribbles down my magenta silk blouse, threatening ruin. I leave the dining room, climb up to the third-floor attic-like bedroom which is tucked above the staircase. Young members are given these rooms, as the climb is steep. It is pitch dark in the hallways, and I could really use a flashlight. I enter the room and grope for the light switch. Lights on, I take off my blouse and run the water in the tiny bedroom sink. Up the drain, a kind of black insect-like creature squiggles out, and it gets bigger and bigger. A grotesque black vein is growing and creeps toward me. I freeze. I can't help it, I scream so loud that the whole lodge can hear me. You would think I was being murdered. Normally I am not a hysterical woman, but the emergence of this creature got the best of me. I'm terrified.

Men come pounding up the stairs, ducking as they arrive in the bedroom doorway. There I am without my shirt on, crowded in this tiny room as I try to explain what I saw. One tall friend came armed with a bat net. I laugh now when I think of it. My hero with a bat net.

Indeed, when I had turned on the light, a bat that was in our bedroom had taken refuge in the drain of the sink. It was the unfolding of the wing emerging from the drain that had given me the shivers of horror. It was then I realized that the rumours about Queen Elizabeth were correct. She and the prince had fled Pennask in the middle of the night to escape the bats in her room. A rumour I now believe is true and verified.

It will be hard to fall asleep that night, but I carefully place a bottle of red wine blocking the drain: Portfolio from Laughing Stock. It is one expensive drain stopper. We giggle as we settle into our twin beds — mine on the far wall, well away from the sink. The taste of tart and sweet linger in our mouths as we dream about our next day's big catch.

SECOND PLACE — **NONFICTION**

History and hearsay come together nicely in this recounting of a visit to a fabled fishing lodge. The writer has an eye and ear for the details that evoke a place and time. The image of moon and fog in a night that is almost too quiet works very well to portend the creepy discovery of a bat in the sink (and a surprising story about the late Queen). Nicely done.

— Theresa Kishkan

SORROW'S OWN ARIA

NATALIE J. CHAN

The Undertaker sings her best today. As usual, it is for an audience of one. She works quickly and efficiently, gently and lovingly, as she cleans the body that was delivered from the hospital morgue yesterday morning. The body is of a woman in her early forties. Nondescript. She has brown hair, with streaks of grey. Average weight, average height. Stretch marks around the belly. A mother. Reason for death? The Undertaker slides her hand down the dead woman's arm until she reaches the wrist. Gingerly, she twists it slightly to reveal the stiff stitches binding the ugly, jagged gash. Already knowing this was a case of suicide from the accompanying hospital file, the Undertaker's breath still catches in surprise.

Today, she feels like Puccini. *Madama Butterfly? Yes*, she thinks. That feels right. She chooses the aria, *One Fine Day.* It always makes her cry to sing it. At this moment, she is in a raw but pensive mood. She looks down at the body's pale bluish skin, cold and hard under her hand, and finds comfort and familiarity. Usually, she is glad for the silent company, but today she wishes it wasn't so silent. Today she wishes for many things…

Yesterday afternoon, the Undertaker had received a package from the private investigation firm. She had known for a bit that the report was complete, and now, finally, it had come through. They had found her daughter. Slow and purposeful, she'd sliced open the crisp manila envelope. She could feel the thickness and weight of it, corroborating the importance of the information held within. It was still cool from sitting out in her mailbox. Her hands had started to shake, and so she quickly ripped the rest of the opening.

She pulled out its contents. "Grace Georgiana Smith," she read out, whisper-quiet, her voice caressing each syllable. It hurt as her daughter's name passed her lips for the first time in over forty years. It was the type of hurt as if someone decided to squeeze their hand around her heart and dig their ragged nails into its very core, without any intention of letting up or letting go. "Georgiana Smith," she said in wonder. Someone must have given her these other names. A seed of resentment began to germinate in the pit of her stomach, but she quickly crushed the feeling. She had no right to be possessive.

She started to sift through. There were photocopies of newspaper clippings. *BABY GIRL FOUND IN CARDBOARD BOX. BABY ABANDONED IN FRONT OF THE H.M. GRANT HOSPITAL. ABANDONED BABY FOUND WITH NOTE.* None of the clippings revealed what the note said, but she remembered. She had written it fretfully after bathing, dressing, and placing her daughter in that shabby box. *Please take my baby. Her name is Grace. I can't take care of her and she needs a chance. There is only me and I am not enough.*

Following the clippings was the investigator's pieced-together story of her daughter. The Undertaker couldn't help but read quickly, so starved was she to receive any news. She forced herself to slow her pace lest she skip over any one of the precious words. The officialness and structure of the neat black letters against the pristine white of the bond paper belied the chaos that was Grace's life. The Undertaker's heart, already squeezed by that unrelenting invisible hand, was going to rupture. *Removed from yet another foster home… difficult time in school… drugs… petty crime… abusive partners… moved to several cities… put her baby up for adoption in Toronto…* The Undertaker closed her eyes and saw those words reflected on the back of her lids. *Put her baby up for adoption in Toronto.* How could all the things she thought she was saving her daughter from come to pass? She knew. Desperation sometimes initiates boldness. She had stepped forward to play fate's game of chance and lost.

She read on… *attempt at a new beginning… moved to Vancouver… new job… change of name…* Change of name? Puzzled and slightly unsettled by this new detail, the Undertaker read her daughter's new name aloud. It rolled off her tongue easily, as if she was already accustomed to it. A long pause followed, and then there was a faint click in her brain. She stood up abruptly, jostling the table and causing her cup of tea to tip over the edge and splinter as it hit the tiled floor. She started to run, and in her panic, she had cut the bottoms of her feet from the shards of porcelain on the ground. She ran across the room and down two flights of stairs, leaving a thick trail of blood. Unlocking the heavy door separating her living quarters from her business, she sprinted to her office down the hallway. She froze at the doorway after noticing the hospital file on her desk. Having received a woman's body earlier that day, she had left the file casually open after review. It rested there now with all its secrets laid bare. *Oh god… dear god…* She didn't have to read through the report again. She just knew. *A mother's instinct?* The Undertaker had laughed ferociously and bitterly at the irony of that thought.

Time passed in anguished seconds and minutes, and maybe longer, as the Undertaker stood in her office doorway. At some point, she turned around and trudged back up the two flights of stairs, ignoring the patches of blood on each step and the pain emanating from the soles of her feet. She sat down heavily on a stool in her kitchen after retrieving the investigation report off the floor. Soggy and fragile from the spilt tea, the *Grace Georgiana Smith* papers were cradled in her lap. She was still and quiet, listening until the early-evening noises of the neighbourhood — the hum of passing cars, children's laughter from the playground, neighbours catching up — gave way to the lonely silence of the latest part of the night. Only the occasional bark of a dog punctured the quiet eeriness.

The Undertaker made her way to bed. She knew she would not sleep. Body preparation was scheduled for the next day and she did not know how she would manage. All she knew was that she would do her best. Her last thought as she closed the lights in her kitchen was one of deep understanding and profound regret. She *would* have been enough. It was too late to know for certain, as that path was severed the moment she left that box on the hospital steps.

There was a small tug on the edge of her thoughts, and she realized that actually, she hadn't come to the end of *all* paths. It wasn't too late to play fate's game of chance once more. The Undertaker bowed her head and made a final decision as she mechanically drew her bedroom curtains to a close. She would contact the private investigator in the morning and ask for another report. She'll tell them to start their search in Toronto.

Honorable Mention — **Fiction**

I immediately fell for this title and the story lived up to that promise. The most straightforward of the three finalists, it has both the practicality of the work the narrator undertakes, and a melancholic air for the person who spends so much time alone with her regrets. Yet there is hope in the end, a faint one. I am a sucker for redemption, and this delivers it.

— Chris (C.C.) Humphreys

SIPPING **COFFEE** FROM A **LEAKY** THERMOS

WENDY WESEEN

alone in the night air. hanging out of a car window on
    Knutsford
road south of Kamloops. Waiting for promised shooting stars
to streak tails across the sky. sipping coffee from a leaky
    thermos infused
with hundred-percent cream and artificial sweetener.

frog songs announce survival. claim midnight in a world of
    extinction.
a single coyote cleaved with the moon. howled. wounding the
    wind.
millions of stars pinprick the air like a 1912 general store tin
    ceiling.
without falling stars and my dead husband. my colonized

body curled around you. soft breasts against your cool back
hand underlining your chest. thighs angle-bent around.
your buttocks taking my breath away.
I slipped into sleep with the howling of memory.

SECOND PLACE — **POETRY**

The stark realization of bringing in contemporary memory of sitting on back roads south of Kamloops, listening to frog songs, and drinking coffee creamer bring the reader right next to the poet. The words speak to revolution through love, shooting stars, companionship while animals serenading the promise of future through a dreamscape. I'm never much for titles but "Sipping Coffee from a Leaky Thermos" is such a perfect way to frame a poem like this. We've all had our own leaky thermos and know the fragility of that. We've all had our own memories of how we hope love can take us somewhere better.

— Conor Kerr

PILGRIMAGE TO THE PAST

DEANNA BARNHARDT KAWATSKI

Why am I going? What can I possibly achieve by visiting the wilderness homestead ten years after the death of our dream? It is seven years since I set foot in the Ningunsaw Valley. It is also seven years since the death of my good friend Denis, who was part of our northern life. As I set out, I half wonder whether his spirit will visit us in the valley.

To begin our pilgrimage, my daughter Natalia and I endure a twenty-two-hour bus marathon from Shuswap Lake to Kitwanga, the northernmost Greyhound bus stop in north-western British Columbia. Natalia was born and lived her first twelve years north of Kitwanga, in the woods to which we now travel.

Natalia isn't only visiting our past; she's also staking a claim for her future. She intends to spend regular intervals in her childhood home. Since our departure a decade ago, a series of renters have drifted through our old homestead, but it has been empty for more than one year. Now it is August and the height of bear season. We have no idea what we will find when we hike in.

We catch a ride the remaining one hundred and twenty miles north of Stewart, where we overnight with friends, and are dropped off at an old logging site. Grabbing my gear and hopping from the truck, I scarcely recognize my surroundings. Time has healed the clear-cut wound, and a profusion of birch, poplar, alder, and pine trees populate what I remember as a moonscape.

The minute Wade rumbles away, my heart lurches as the tall grass ahead parts and something rushes directly towards us. I blink my eyes at the sight of an exquisite red fox. His gait seems urgent, almost as though he is expecting us. Evidently a male, he is rust red with a darker hue running the length of his back and along his lavish tail. Judging by his size, he was born this past year. Nat and I freeze, mesmerized. He bounds closer and closer until he is near enough to touch. His enormous ears are perked; his bright brown eyes study us with an uncanny intensity. As though trying to entice us to play, he lopes around us in a circle. We are baffled by his behaviour, since he looks in perfect health and there is no one nearby to have tamed him. I remember that, during his last lonely months, Denis had a fox friend who became his quiet joy. My friend's empty hut is only two miles from where we now stand.

The fox is in no hurry to leave, and as Nat rearranges her pack for the hike, he performs his full repertoire of tricks. With all of my years in the bush, I have never been this close to a wild fox; I can't keep my eyes off him. He scratches his ear for a bit, then he drags his butt along the ground. I'm amazed as he sinks to the clover-covered ground, rests his head on his paws and stares at me long and hard. I feel honoured by his presence. Even with the string of jingle bells I now tie around my ankles, to alert bears to our presence, he lingers. As we hoist our packs and set out, the fox dances along behind us; when I glance back again, he is gone.

We fall into a rhythm, walking the two miles to where our trail plunges four hundred feet into the valley. Worming our way through the lush growth, we notice frequent bear sign. Both black bears and grizzlies inhabit this region, and can be aggressive when surprised. We announce our presence by singing with vigour, "I love to go a'wandering…" and "I gave my love a cherry that has no stone…" Here and there, huge footprints mark the mud. I grow a bit uneasy.

A breeze blows the bugs away as we clamber down the hill through the trees and thimbleberry bushes. Memories of many past hikes with small children come to mind. "Wait for me," rings in my ears from long ago. Now, I struggle to keep up with Nat. On the final two hundred foot, ligament-snapping slope, I quiver from the exertion and with anticipation of what we will find at the bottom. Nat calls back to me through a screen of silver poplar, "I see smoke!"

"Wait for me!" I holler. Negotiating the last stretch of the hill, I obtain a clear view of the parcel of wilderness that consumed thirteen years of my life.

Surprised, I spot Joe, an old family friend who sometimes checks on the place. He's waiting for us in the front yard, spry at sixty-six in his T-shirt, sweat pants, and gumboots; we greet each other warmly.

I survey the collapsed fence along the hill and chunks of bark strewn in front of the house. My heart sinks at the signs of neglect. The stovepipe at the back of the log house is askew; the back door is blocked by cottonwood saplings. When we lived here, we took pride in tending the house and gardens. I see that in front of the kitchen window, wild crimson elderberries have shoved out the pansies and forget-me-nots that once bloomed.

Twisting the burl doorknob, we enter the kitchen. Everything looks smaller than I remember — and dingy. I feel like I have outgrown it. My Findlay oval wood cook stove used to sit centre stage in the kitchen. When it was stolen seven years ago — airlifted by helicopter — it was as though someone had ripped the heart out of the house. More recently, one of the renters moved a small cast iron heater up from the cabin built by Philip and Roy from Berlin. Now the house has a small heart but at least it is still ticking. I have a special relationship with this squat stove. It kept me warm in the German cabin throughout the long months that I began to write *Wilderness Mother*.

In a corner of the kitchen, Joe has rigged up a mousetrap, using a bucket, string, and a peanut butter-smeared-can. "I caught thirty last night," he says.

He suggests a walk to the pond. My memory of the pond is a brown muck hole. *The dam had burst. The water was gone.* As we scamper down the hill, we pass the wooden bear that Jay carved over twenty years ago. Standing on the lip of the old dam, Natalia and I gawk with confusion. The pond is back! We drink in the reflected view, embraced by tall swamp grass.

Venturing farther east, we see where the beaver has repaired the hole in the dam by filling it with birch and poplar limbs and packing it with a mortar of mud. We follow a trail he has trampled up the north bank and directly into the old chicken yard. Pale poplar stumps glow against the ground. Nat and I cheer the work of the beaver.

As we cross the footbridge, I notice below, at the edge of Natty Creek, the turquoise turbine that Denis built for us in 1989. I feel fresh horror as I remember his fate.

We wander to the old garden site. Where once orderly rows of vegetables prospered and fed a family of four, a northern jungle now grows. In its midst, we find devil's club, stinging nettle, and the valour of rhubarb, its ruddy stalks still holding strong under the siege of elderberry. A few feet away, a colony of saffron-coloured lilies proclaim their allegiance to the past, when masses of their kind bloomed in multihued glory. Near Natty Creek, which snakes the length of the clearing, we find frail asparagus ferns in the grasp of fecund wild growth. As we fight our way to the most westerly part of the garden, the mosquitoes swell in numbers. Here, a healthy patch of comfrey still sprawls in the grass among cow parsnips. I am touched to see that nature has allowed a few remnants of our past life to remain.

Joe leaves in the evening, and knowing that we only have five days here, Natalia and I decide to ignore our watches and descend back into sacred time, the endless cycle of seasons and nature, unfazed by man's time machines.

The next day is overcast. Every crook and corner of the house is filthy. Nat scampers around like a squirrel sweeping, scrubbing, and straightening. I yank the plastic storm window from above the sink, and, loathing dirty windowsills, I scrub this one where I used to set fresh raspberry and huckleberry pies to cool. Perpetually seized by scenes from the past, I see a tiny Nat in quilted overalls and bright sweater dancing down the giant cottonwood-crowded trail, and two-year-old Ben, in royal blue velour, high stepping it across the pine-plank floor.

We take a break from cleaning and amble to the creek with buckets to fetch water that no longer flows to the house. As I scoop a bucketful, I become caught up in the incantations of the sparkling stream. Resting before carrying it back up the hill, I hug a huge spruce tree. Pressing my ear against the puzzling texture, I feel as though I could access the creation story of the entire universe. Yesterday I wondered how we survived such an isolated existence. Today I remember.

After lugging the buckets up to the house, I wander back down the hill to harvest some rhubarb. As I gaze out across the tangled garden, I imagine the spirit of Denis standing below. Beside him lingers a red fox. Their images merge in my mind.

Denis the Menace, I called him. Practical joker, chain smoker with nicotine-gold fingertips. I can see him standing there, his grubby hat pulled low, a perpetual mug of coffee in his hand, his checked shirt untucked on one side. He fires another wisecrack at me, followed by his incessant giggle.

I first met Denis in 1980 and got to know him through a series of visits he paid to our Ningunsaw Valley homestead. He admired our lifestyle and was attempting something similar south, up the Bell Irving River. This proved to be a place of power for him, because it was where he learned to produce hydroelectricity. Denis built his first turbine there, carving it out of balsam with a chainsaw. After visiting him, my ex-husband reported that Denis hadn't built a cabin yet, but he had a light bulb swinging from the trees and a fan to blow the bugs away. I was struck by the ingenuity of a man to whom life had dealt some bitter blows.

Born in Schumacher, Ontario in 1951 to a French Canadian family, Denis lost his mother, then his father. He said he would never forget what his uncle said to him at his father's funeral. "You're a man now. You'll have to look after yourself." Denis was fifteen years old. His siblings were scattered throughout foster homes while he hit the road hitchhiking through Canada and the United States. He never had contact with any family members again.

Denis found work in logging camps in backwoods BC, and in the evening he taught himself English by reading western paperbacks. Later, he became a high-paid diamond driller, thereby tasting affluence for a few years. But he was much more acquainted with the sting of poverty. Returning to the logging industry, a blow from a tree left him with a damaged back and chronic pain. Despite his valid case and best efforts, which included a winter of haunting the Workmen's Compensation Board office in downtown Vancouver, he never received a bean.

When Denis visited, his arrival was invariably humble, his presence shining. Even though he was as poor as a wharf rat, he always came bearing gifts. He came for Christmas when Natalia was three years old, and he showed up with what was, for her, a most exotic present — a white-and-yellow tea set, with which she served her entourage of dolls for many seasons. "Can I have your big toe for my trophy wall?" he'd tease Nat. "No, you can't because it's got bones in it!" she'd say. Her reply always sent him into a seizure of giggles.

For years, we urged Denis to settle in the Ningunsaw Valley and he shyly declined. However, he visited frequently. More than willing to pitch in with whatever project was in progress, he chipped away at the hillside above the pond with a pickaxe, and manoeuvred the rock and soil downhill to our dam in a homemade wheelbarrow as long as his back could stand it. Over the years, he loaned a huge hand to the development of our hydroelectric system.

What Denis and I shared as our friendship matured was philosophical conversation and whoops of laughter. His presence lit up what could be a lonely life. With little more than grade eight education, he considered himself to be a simple man. To put it in his own words: "Being not too bright of a guy. Being strong like bull and smart like street car." His motto was *KISS*, standing for "keep it simple, stupid". Yet how many university graduates ever become fluent in *kilowatese* to the point of creating electricity from scraps cast off by our society?

Denis also became mesmerized by computers, and through a mail-order course, he learned not only how to program them, but also how to repair and even build them. Yes, Denis went disk drive, and you needed to know cyberspace to even talk to him. Everything was either in kilowatts or megabytes.

I bumped into him in Stewart one winter, and he worried me. He was as wired as a snowshoe hare with its tail in a socket. His eyes red from amazement exhaustion, he had been surfing the net for three days and three nights. With his expertise, he helped several Stewart businesses convert to computers. And whenever he needed to escape from town, he'd thumb a ride out and pitch in with the work in exchange for a bed and some good home cooking.

One afternoon as I kneaded the bread dough, Denis sauntered over and told me that someone had invented an electric bread maker. You poured all of your ingredients in, he said, then lifted out a perfect brown loaf. "Yeah sure, Denis." I refused to get sucked in this time. I had been making our own bread from scratch for ten years, right down to grinding our own wheat grown below in the garden. How could anyone be so irreverent as to shortcut this wholesome and meditative practise? I'll never forget his hearty laugh at the look on my face when I learned that he was telling the truth for a change.

What outshone Denis's perpetually inquiring mind was his heart of gold. His greatest quality was his capacity to care for others, and even though he had next to nothing, he always found ways to give.

After the kids and I settled at Shuswap Lake, Denis supported me in phone calls and letters, including a fifteen-page handwritten one. In 1993 he set up his own little house in the bush four miles down the Ningunsaw River from our homestead. He threw himself into producing hydroelectricity, fuelled by his dream of building a one-thousand-square-foot greenhouse. My life surged on, caught up in the whirl of seeing my own dream materialize in the form of my book, *Wilderness Mother*. Even as my desire to return to the north dwindled, Denis pushed on with his plans. Not having the money to buy pipe, he built penstocks out of lumber, cutting all of the necessary boards with his chainsaw. This long, elaborate system of wooden troughs connected the forty-foot-wide, seven-foot-tall dam with his pride and joy — the turbine in his wheelhouse.

We visited Denis at his new hut in May, 1995. I was shocked by how unhealthy he looked. He was leaning on Tylenol 3s to save him from endless back pain, and his main diet was still coffee and cigarettes.

On January 22, 1996, I received terrible news from my friend Pat in Stewart. Denis was dead. He had somehow gotten his arm caught in the step-up drive of his water power system. It was −45 degrees Celsius when they found him, and no one knew how long he had been gone.

For me far away at Shuswap Lake, Denis had come to symbolize the Ningunsaw and life in the north. It was ironical that he moved to the bush after our family fell apart and fled. Denis had kept a light burning, one created by his own ingenuity. Now the last light had gone out in the Ningunsaw Valley.

A particular coincidence astonished me; my daughter Natalia had been born near the creek flowing into Desire Lake, while Denis had died beside the creek flowing out of Desire Lake. *The world breathes in and someone is born. The world breathes out and someone dies.* I remember that Denis's ashes were spread here in the Ningunsaw Valley, now resonating around me.

The spell is broken by the cry of a raven, and I pull enough rhubarb stalks for sauce, and back at the house, set it on the wood stove to stew; the place soon fills with a nostalgic aroma. Nat and I laugh a lot, and tears also fall for what was lost, for how things might have been. No matter what, we were lucky to have experienced a life about which most people only dream. We achieved a substantial degree of self-sufficiency in a peaceful and wild setting, unencumbered by civilization.

Later in the afternoon, we realize that no visit to the valley would be complete without a hike to the Ningunsaw River. For thirteen years, it flowed through my dreams and lured us out to play. Just beyond the garden, we encounter a new stream and cross it on a network of slippery logs. Quickly we become submerged in wild growth; the acrid smell of cow parsnips and devil's club fills our nostrils. I recognize remnants of the old path beneath my feet. Breaking loose of the timber, we greet the mountains on the south side of the Ningunsaw River. We wind our way through fireweed and cottonwood seedlings to a carpet of fine, black sand. The green glacial water churns past, and I scan it with sober respect, remembering the summer I crossed with a sprained knee and was nearly swept away.

We wander downstream eyeing wolf prints. I tense as we encounter bear tracks — a small set traces the lip of the river, and a larger set of grizzly tracks meanders towards the jagged peaks, west across the Iskut River. Reluctantly leaving the open flat, we clamber back through the brush. As we approach the house, the hair on the back of my neck prickles at the sight of steaming, pink bear scat dropped near the garden during our walk to the river. We peer around but the visitor is gone.

In the evening, Nat and I sip wild mint tea on the front porch — one of my favourite places on earth. I watch the slow dance of magenta fireweed. From this vantage point in earlier times, we observed the antics of moose, bears, and wolves. Now nature has reclaimed the clearing in a wild way, and we stand little chance of spotting anything. The south-facing porch has grown rickety, with spots only a fool would dare stand on — it is a forty-foot drop to the creek.

I find myself "watching" my younger self. I feel the tumbling ahead of my own life even as I watch the small but determined dark-haired woman crouch to weed two-hundred-foot rows of vegetables. Two beautiful blonde children help. A tanned man with a blonde beard swings the sickle and cuts golden wheat.

I see the same dark head bowed over a scrub board balanced in a tub at the edge of a creek. Her eyes lift, widen and assess the situation as a fat black bear raises its snout and stares at her from its resting place on the hillside eight feet away. She shouts; slowly, it rises and ambles on.

Birch and cottonwood leaves now shiver around us. With a rush of emotion I feel great sadness for Denis; followed by forgiveness and even affection for who we all were then. With noble intentions, we set out to create our own world and to lead a simple life of self-sufficiency and harmony with nature. And we largely achieved that. Yet how naive of us to think that we could survive forever without the balancing energy of a like-minded community. We had no neighbours to support us when times were especially challenging. Denis had moved to the Ningunsaw too late. Yet what a prominent part this valley played in shaping who I am today! Since leaving, I've echoed its voice in writing two books. The lessons that I learned here — patience, perseverance, humility, reverence, a deep sense of my own purpose and a greater capacity to love — gave me the courage to embark upon a whole new life.

Mosquitoes sing and poke at my ears. In the distance, I hear the roar of the Ningunsaw River. With a surge of insight, I understand how important it is for us to honour the sacred places, people, and moments of our lives. In a society obsessed with "getting over it" and "getting on with it," acknowledging one's own past as a teacher is crucial to completing the circles.

I needed to return to reclaim bits of my soul that I dropped on my flight out of here. Now I see that some of it will remain here forever. I needed to return to pay tribute to Denis. I needed to return to meet the red fox. Forever in my mind's eyes, his wild being will glow as he lopes along the ridgeline between the waking and spirit world.

AUTHORS AND **JUDGES**

Andrew Buckley is a film school-educated writer, which means he's spent most of his life with no money and a high opinion about bad movies. Sometime around the turn of the century, he attended the Vancouver Film School's Writing for Film and Television program, graduating with excellence. He pitched and developed several screenplay projects before turning to his chosen career of novel writing (this was due, in part, to his discovery that 'professional mongoose wrangler' wasn't a real profession).

As a writer, Andrew favors playing in the fantasy and paranormal sandboxes and is drawn to writing with a humorous and satirical slant despite being asked politely on numerous occasions to 'please stop doing that'. As the co-founder and lead instructor at Wordsmith Academy, Andrew speaks to thousands of students each year about storytelling and writing through the delivery of interactive and engaging workshops and presentations at schools, writing conferences, and comic cons.

Finnian Burnett teaches undergrad composition, creative writing, and early British Lit. They are addicted to very small stories, and their recent flash fiction collection, *The Clothes Make the Man*, was recently published by Ad Hoc Fiction. Finn has been published through Reflex Press, *Ekphrastic Review*, *Pulp Literature*, *Blank Spaces Magazine*, *Daily Science Fiction*, and more. A second novella-in-flash, *The Price of Cookies*, is forthcoming through Off Topic Publishing. Finn is currently working on a collection of queer love stories and a *Star Trek*-themed flash fiction collection. They live in British Columbia with their spouse and with Lord Gordo, the cat.

Serena Caner is a registered dietitian and Executive Director of a local non-profit organization, Shuswap Food Action Society. She moved to the Shuswap with her husband in 2008 and has two wonderful daughters. In her spare time, she loves creative writing. To date, she exclusively publishes her works in the *Askew's Word on the Lake Anthology*.

Natalie J. Chan writes short pieces, stories for children, poems, and reminder lists for her two forgetful teens. Tidbits of novels, plots, and character ideas can be found on sticky notes and doggy-eared journals that litter her bedside table. An enthusiast of various genres, what she writes about and how she goes about it change like the seasons. The one constant in her ever-shifting creative process is her love of telling a good story.

Natalie has a master's in business administration and pursued a career in human resources until she decided to take a wholesale parenting break. She lives in Toronto exploring fresh life goals with her supportive husband and children.

Scott Fitzgerald Gray (9th-level layabout, vindictive good) is a writer of fantasy and speculative fiction, a fiction editor, a story editor, and an editor and designer of roleplaying games — all of which means he finally has the job he really wanted when he was sixteen. He shares his life in the Canadian hinterland with a schoolteacher, two itinerant daughters, and a number of animal and spirit companions. More info on him and his work (some of it even occasionally truthful) can be found by reading between the lines at insaneangel.com.

Scott was the editor of the *Askew's Word on the Lake Anthology 2023*.

Caitlin Hicks is the author of the 2015 novel *A Theory of Expanded Love*, which won many awards, including IndieFAB Bronze (now Foreword Indies) and iTunes for Best New Fiction. In 2022, the novel won listing on BookRiot's list of 100 Must-Read Books about Women and Religion, alongside celebrated writers Alice Walker, Barbara Kingsolver, Toni Morrison, Arundhati Roy, Margaret Atwood, Ann Patchett, Alice Hoffman, and more. The audiobook of *A Theory of Expanded Love* won the NYC Big Book Award as a Distinguished Favorite in 2022.

Hicks is also an international playwright and acclaimed performer. Her theatrical writing has been performed in *Best Women's Stage Monologues* (New York), *SheSpeaks* (Playwrights Canada Press), and the Canadian Broadcasting Corporation's national radio. A screen adaptation of Hicks's internationally toured play *Singing the Bones* debuted as a feature film at Montreal World Film Festival (2001) and screened around the world.

Hicks's writing has been published in the *Vancouver Sun*, the *Los Angeles Times*, the *San Francisco Chronicle*, the *Milwaukee Journal Sentinel*, *The Fiddlehead*, and other publications. Her podcast *Some Kinda Woman — Stories of Us*, captures women's voices at small and profound moments in their lives. Learn more at CaitlinHicks.com.

Chris (C.C.) Humphreys — born in Toronto, raised in London — is a third-generation actor and writer who has played Hamlet in Calgary, a gladiator in Tunisia, waltzed in London's West End, conned the landlord of the Rovers Return in *Coronation Street*, patrolled the Sun Hill beat in *The Bill*, commanded a starfleet in *Andromeda*, voiced Salem the cat in the original *Sabrina*, and is a dead immortal in *Highlander*.

He has written four plays and twenty-one novels, including *The French Executioner*, runner-up for the CWA Steel Dagger for Thrillers; *Chasing the Wind*; *The Jack Absolute Trilogy*, recently reissued; *Vlad — The Last Confession*; *A Place Called Armageddon*; and *Shakespeare's Rebel* — which he adapted into a play and which premiered at Bard on the Beach, Vancouver, in 2015. *Plague* won the Arthur Ellis Award for Best Crime Novel in Canada in 2015.

He has an MFA in Creative Writing from the University of British Columbia. He is now writing epic fantasy with the *Immortals' Blood Trilogy*, for Gollancz. He has also just published his other new fantasy series, *The Tapestry Trilogy*, beginning with *The Hunt of the Unicorn*. His most recent novel is *One London Day*, a modern thriller. June 2023 will see the publication of his WW2 thriller, *Someday I'll Find You*. He lives on Salt Spring Island, BC.

Chris was the fiction judge for the 2023 Askew's Word on the Lake Writing Contest.

Evan J (he/they) has spent the last decade living in Toronto, Ottawa, and Sioux Lookout, Ontario. Evan's first book, *Ripping down half the trees*, was published in 2021 with McGill-Queen's University Press. Currently, Evan is the fiction editor for *Cloud Lake Literary* journal, the programming coordinator of the Winnipeg International Writers Festival, and a facilitator of poetry writing workshops across Ontario and Manitoba for Vallum's Poetry for Our Future! program. When living in Ottawa, Evan learned to write poetry. When living in Toronto, Evan ran Slackline Creative Arts Series, a popular reading series and collective that showcased emerging writers and artists. When living in Sioux Lookout, Evan taught creative writing and 3D printing to Indigenous adults living in remote First Nations. Now living in Winnipeg, Evan primarily writes fiction.

Deanna Barnhardt Kawatski is the author of the bestselling memoirs *Wilderness Mother* (Lyons & Burford, New York) and *Clara and Me* (Whitecap Books), a BC Book Prize nominee; plus the novel *Stalking the Wild Heart* (Gracesprings Collective), a travel memoir called *Burning Man, Slaying Dragon,* the children's books *Samira, the Singing Salmon* and *Big Trees Saved* (Shuswap Press). Most recently she has released *My Life Is in Your Hand (The many loves of Sophia, a Norwegian rebel & Shuswap pioneer),* and *Magda's Odyssey,* a YA novel whose audiobook version she narrated in collaboration with CKVS, Voice of the Shuswap. She lives in the North Shuswap, where her roots reach back over one hundred years.

In 1978, Deanna worked as a forestry lookout attendant in the remote reaches of northwestern BC, where she met her hermit husband. For the next thirteen years, she led the life of a pioneering mother in the wilderness. At the same time, she wrote feature articles for many magazines including *Mother Earth News* (to which she became a contributing editor), *Harrowsmith, Canadian Gardening, Country Journal,* and *Outdoor Canada.*

Deanna is a popular workshop presenter and has given over one hundred public readings including at the Vancouver International Writers' Festival. She worked as a writer-in-residence at the Ryga Centre in 2002 and has been a director of the Word on the Lake Writers' Festival since its inception. Deanna is featured on the first-ever Literary Map of BC. Visit her website at deannabkawatski.com.

Conor Kerr is a Métis/Ukrainian writer. A member of the Métis Nation of Alberta, he is descended from the Lac Ste. Anne Métis and the Papaschase Cree Nation. His Ukrainian family are settlers in Treaty 4 and 6 territories in Saskatchewan. His writing has been awarded the 2021 *Malahat Review*'s Long Poem Prize and the 2020 *Fiddlehead*'s Ralph Gustafson Award. He was named one of CBC's 2022 Writers to Watch.

He is the author of the poetry collection *An Explosion of Feathers* and the novel *Avenue of Champions*, which was short-listed for the Amazon Canada First Novel Award, longlisted for the 2022 Giller Prize, and won the 2022 ReLIT award. He has a forthcoming poetry book, *Old Gods*, out in Spring 2023 and a novel, *Prairie Edge*, out in 2024.

Conor was the poetry judge for the 2023 Askew's Word on the Lake Writing Contest.

Harrison Kim grew up in the Shuswap and now lives and writes in Victoria, Canada. The story in this anthology appeared in real life before it made it to the page, altered in major aspects, yet with the same theme of that old green-eyed demon jealousy. Harrison Kim's stories have appeared in *Hobart Pulp*, *X Ray Literary Magazine*, *Blue Lake Review*, *Coffin Bell*, *The Horror Zine*, *Bewildering Stories*, *Literally Stories*, and others over the past four years. His blogspot, with publications and video links, is here: https://harrisonkim1.blogspot.com/

Theresa Kishkan lives on the Sechelt Peninsula with her husband, John Pass, in a house they built and where they raised their three children. She has published fourteen books, most recently *Euclid's Orchard*, a collection of essays about family history, botany, mathematics, and love (Mother Tongue Publishing, 2017); a novella, *The Weight of the Heart* (Palimpsest Press,

2020), in which a young graduate student attempts to create a feminist cartography with the works of Ethel Wilson and Sheila Watson; and *Blue Portugal and Other Essays* (University of Alberta Press, 2022), a collection of lyrical essays.

Her books have been nominated for many awards, including the Hubert Evans Award and the Ethel Wilson Prize. Her interests include textiles, ethnobotany, music, human and physical geography, and colour theory, strands of which are braided together in *Blue Portugal*.

Theresa was the nonfiction judge for the 2023 Askew's Word on the Lake Writing Contest.

Kaija Pepper's writing on dance has found a home in many national and international newspapers, magazines, anthologies, journals, and theatre programs. As editor of the now web-based *Dance International*, Kaija appreciates the opportunity to connect with writers from across Canada and around the world. She has recently begun to explore the challenging but rewarding territory of creative nonfiction and memoir. Her 2020 book, *Falling into Flight: A Memoir of Life and Dance* (Signature Editions), was described by *The Georgia Straight* as "terrific storytelling" and "utterly compelling," and "highly recommended" by the *Vancouver Sun*.

Melissa Sawatsky is a writer who currently lives, works and creates on unceded Gidimt'en territory in the Witsuwit'en Nation. She is a communications professional and event coordinator at Smithers Public Library, and serves on the board of the Bulkley Valley Community Arts Council. She also coordinates and facilitates creative writing workshops for youth and adults. Melissa's work has appeared in *Room*, *Poetry is Dead*, *The Maynard*, *Northword*, *Sad Mag*, *The Found Poetry Review*, and *Rhubarb*, among other magazines. Her poetry has also been published in anthologies such as *The Enpipe Line* and *Sustenance: Writers from BC and Beyond on the Subject of Food*. She has a Master of Fine Arts in Creative Writing from the University of British Columbia.

Donna VanSant (Ed.D., M.Sc, B.P.E.) is known for her penchant for innovation and "start-ups." Her animated, inquisitive style encourages others to break out of entrenched patterns and try new approaches. From the position of teacher-leader in the Surrey School District, she established the District Research and Evaluation Department which published *The Research Forum, A Journal Devoted to Educational Practice and Theory*. This journal was distributed to every school in the province of British Columbia for over a decade.

As researcher and writer, Donna practices grounded theory, which is a systemic inductive process of gathering patterns and insight from the lived or "grounded" experience. Currently, she is associate faculty at Royal Roads University (RRU) and president of the African Canadian Continuing Education Foundation (ACCES). She has taught in two school districts and at five universities, and after early retirement, has operated her own company, Healthy Ventures.

Donna was born in Kentucky and now centres her life in three places in British Columbia, Canada: Crescent Beach on the West Coast, CROFT farm in Coldstream, and at the VanSant lake house in the Shuswap.

Wendy Weseen has created visual art most of her life. Fifteen years ago, when she acquired osteoarthritis in her hands, she became unable to create art the way she had been. She began writing travel memoirs, personal essays (four accepted by *The*

Globe and Mail), and poetry, and has been most recently published in *Event Magazine* and by *Repartee Publishing*. She has obtained degrees in humanities, social work, and fine art, and was awarded the Most Distinguished Award for studio art and the Silver Medal in Fine Art from the University of Saskatchewan in 2001. She incorporates diverse themes into both her art and writing, which often contains playful sociological commentaries.

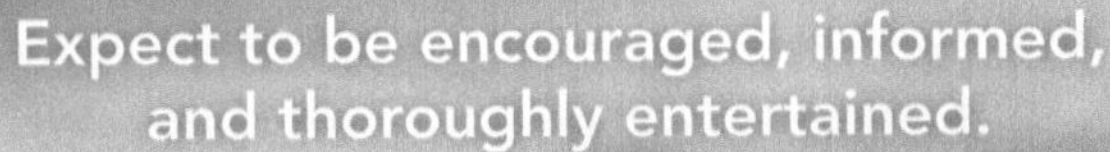

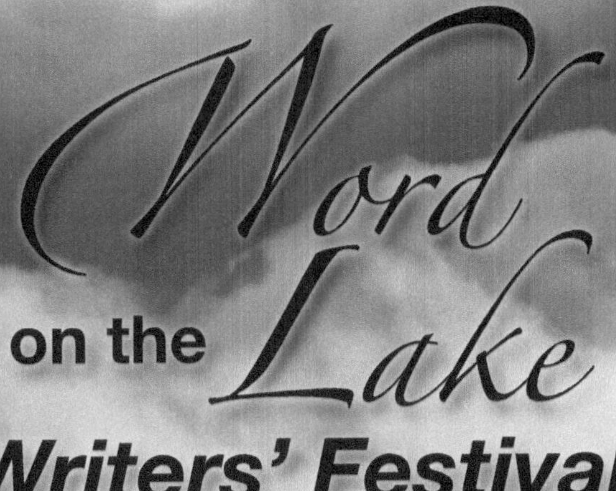

Each year, Word on the Lake brings in a selection
of published authors and industry professionals
from Canada and abroad, for a full weekend of
workshops, presentations, panels, and master classes.

Whatever level of writer you may be,
you'll want to be part of this inspiring weekend
on the shores of spectacular Shuswap Lake.

Go to www.wordonthelakewritersfestival.com for
updates, announcements, and registration.

The Shuswap Association of Writers celebrates the written word!

How do we do that? By:

- Connecting readers and writers with authors and their works
- Organizing the Word on the Lake Writers' Festival — a major literary event in the interior of British Columbia, which brings together writers, readers, published authors, editors, and publishers in an exciting and stimulating weekend festival.
- Promoting literacy in the Shuswap

- Providing relevant workshops in our community related to all aspects of writing
- Promoting authors by arranging public readings
- Working with young writers through the Kidswrite Contest
- Organizing Young Writers workshops
- Providing opportunities for writers to showcase their work through the Askew's Word On The Lake Writing Contest and the Word on the Lake Anthology

Join the Shuswap Association of Writers today and receive registration discounts at SAW-sponsored events, advance notice of regional events, invites to local author book launches, and more!

Go to www.wordonthelakewritersfestival.com/saw/ for information.